OUR ROMAN PASTS

OUR ROMAN PASTS

MICHAEL HARTWIG

Herring Cove Press

Contents

Acknowledgements

Special thanks to Flavia Vittucci, of Rome, Italy, for reviewing the manuscript, checking grammar, correcting Italian phrases, and verifying information about archaeological sites.

Cover Art - Author - "Trajan's Forum"

I

Chapter One – Trajan's Forum

Julian, holding a steaming cup of coffee, leaned against the plaster wall and glanced out of the large open window of his parlor. The morning air was fresh, but he could feel the humidity, foreshadowing a sultry day. Bright sunshine bathed the marble and stone foundations of Trajan's Forum just below his apartment. The cream ribbed Baroque dome of Santissimo Nome di Maria cast a long shadow on the magnificent marble relief column erected at the beginning of the 2nd century to commemorate Trajan's victory over the Dacians. In the near distance, traffic had already begun to snarl Piazza Venezia under the towering monument of Victor Emanuel.

Julian breathed in the distinctive smells of Rome, roasted coffee, pollen, exhaust, and a sweet earthy scent rising from ancient ruins and old buildings. He sensed a bit of salty air from the sea and the faint effervescent aroma of water flowing briskly in the nearby Tiber River.

After securing the window, he returned to the spacious parlor and opened his laptop. There were a couple of emails from lawyers and confirmation of deposits into his accounts. He gazed at a framed photo on the credenza. Marcella was arm in arm with her parents. Piero, dressed in a tailored dark suit, was proud of his beautiful daughter, wearing a laurel wreath for her baccalaureate. Camilla, stunningly beautiful – deep dark eyes, thick lashes, high cheekbones, dark hair, and a caramel silky complexion – seemed distracted, as if something were happening in front of them.

Over the years, Marcella had grown to look more and more like her mother. He picked up the photo and scrutinized her features. She was beautiful as a college student. She had luminous skin, deep set hazel eyes, and a sensuous nose. She had blonde highlights in her brunette hair, and she had an enchanting and affable smile. He ran his fingers affectionately over the photo and then set it back on the table.

Julian rose and walked toward the kitchen. His in-laws had preserved the apartment as a historical residence with antique furniture, lights, drapes, and carpets. Historic paintings covered the walls. The kitchen was the only room that had been modernized – with updated appliances, marble countertops, glass and wood cabinets, and recessed lighting. He grabbed a croissant from a pastry box on the counter, spread some butter and marmalade on it, and returned to the window. He had arrived only a few days before, and the views were mesmerizing. He never tired of looking out over the ancient city, one so different from his home in Atlanta.

Just below his window on the edge of the excavations, a man had set up an easel. It was one of those clever French wooden devices with tripod legs, a hidden compartment for paints, and an adjustable back upon which to lean and secure a canvas. He had another small canvas bag that looked like it held water, fruit, and a sandwich.

Although painters were numerous in Rome, he had never noticed one in front of Trajan's forum. They usually gathered in Piazza Navona, Campo de' Fiori, on the terrace overlooking the Roman Forum, at the top of the Spanish Steps, and in other places with more iconic views.

Julian's building shaded the painter's spot, but he came prepared for the intense sun that would follow. He wore a long-sleeve white shirt, shorts, and had a broad-brimmed straw hat hanging by a cord on his back. As he turned to retrieve something from the canvas bag, Julian glimpsed his face. He fully expected to see a weathered, dark, gritty artist. To his surprise, the man looked as if he could have been a banker or a lawyer. He had a broad forehead and closely cropped dark hair tapered around his temples, ears, and neck. He had a closely trimmed beard that lined his chin and encircled his sensuous mouth. He had an angular face, prominent jaws, and a long but classic nose.

The painter turned back to the easel and reached into another bag, retrieving a canvas that had been prepped with an umber wash. He secured it to the easel and squeezed some oil paint onto a palette. Julian glanced toward the excavations to determine what the artist was planning to paint. There were lines of columns standing on foundations of ancient brick and stone. Most of the columns were plain, without capitals. A few, on the other side of the space, had pieces of architectural detail and carvings still intact.

Julian watched the man step back and contemplate the setting. He then dipped a brush in some paint and made a few tentative strokes on the canvas. Julian walked away from the window and back into the parlor. He sat down again in front of his computer and opened some documents he was studying. He poured another cup of coffee and sat down to work.

An hour later, he walked down a hallway to a small half-bath, peed, and returned to the parlor, stopping at the window to observe the artist. To his surprise, the painting had progressed considerably. The image included a row of columns bathed in the angular morning light. The line of columns converged with a line of pines on the far edge of the archaeological site, creating a natural triangular shape on the canvas.

Julian loved umbrella pines. They had been cultivated to shade old Roman roads, their tall trunks branching high in the sky to form a dense canopy. They seemed to have their own personalities, no two alike. The painter had captured the contrast between the darker green undersides and the lighter tops where the sun illuminated the branches. He had depicted the trees with all their imperfections, including the irregular shifts and angles of the trunks and the quirky and delicate branches holding up cascading clumps of green. Julian noted the way the artist had depicted the golden morning light as it was caught in the rough bark. These seemed to mirror yet contrast with the columns, erect, straight, and uniform. He had captured the slanting morning sunlight, casting some columns lighter and others in shadow. One could almost sense movement in the play of light on the inert structures.

Julian was mouth agape. In just an hour, the painter had brought the scene to life. The incline of sunlight, the contrasting shadows, and the lines and details were stunning. Although he had contemplated the exact same scene hundreds of times before, he had never seen it in such richness. It was as if he had seen it for the first time - the lines, details, and orientation staged dramatically in the pigment and hues the artist had chosen.

Julian ordinarily refrained from watching painters near their place of work. He feared he would break the spell they seemed to be under as they made scenes appear as if by magic. Concealed in his third-floor perch, he observed the artist mix paint to create unique hues and shades of color. He was fascinated by the selection of brushes, some tight for delicate lines and others rough and loose for texture.

He watched the man mix what looked like umber with vermilion, crimson, and white to create the distinctive look of old Roman brick that was exposed after previous generations took the protective marble away to build Renaissance churches and palaces.

As the sun rose, the artist's spot grew brighter and warmer. He placed his hat on his head and pulled out a bottle of water from his bag, sat on a nearby bench, and took generous sips of water. He gazed at the painting, tilted his head, looked out over the ruins, and then stood to make several corrections to the painting. He stepped back from the canvas and made a few more strokes.

He returned to the bench and opened a sandwich. He rolled back the sleeves of his shirt and crossed his legs. They were muscular, dark, and covered in soft black hair. His forearms were strong, extending out from broad shoulders. Despite the heat, he seemed relaxed, serene, and graceful in his earlier movement from palette to canvas, almost as if he were dancing.

As the sun rose higher in the sky and the heat became sultry and intense, Julian noticed the painter begin to pack his easel with supplies and the wet canvas. He wrapped wet brushes in a rag, covered the palette, and slid the canvas into a special carrying case. He slipped the strap of the smaller canvas bag over his shoulder and walked toward Piazza Venezia, where he smoothly navigated traffic and disappeared into the neighborhood on the other side of the square.

Julian decided to go out for lunch. He had just arrived in Rome, and he still enjoyed reclaiming old haunts. He rinsed his face, brushed his hair, grabbed his keys and wallet, and ran down the large marble stairs out onto the street below. He glanced toward the excavations and watched the steady stream of tourist make their way toward the Colosseum further down the boulevard. He turned in the opposite direction and made his way through a maze of small streets into the historical center.

There was a small trattoria he loved, set in an airy square formed by the irregular placement of several 15th century buildings. The restaurant had a pleasant terrace with tables set in the natural shade formed by the overhanging eaves of the historic structures.

"*Ah, Professor Phillips! Bentornato,*" the maître d' said as he recognized Julian approaching the front door.

"*Angelo, che piacere! Da quanto tempo,*" Julian replied, acknowledging that it had been some time since he had last been in Rome.

"I'm sorry to hear about Mrs. Phillips," Angelo said in rough English, placing his hand affectionately on Julian's shoulder.

"Thank you. It was a long ordeal. She's at peace."

Angelo nodded and then pointed to a table on the edge of the terrace.

Julian opened the menu but already knew what he wanted – veal scallopini, peas, and porcini mushroom risotto. Angelo returned with water, and Julian asked for a half bottle of a local red wine and placed his order.

This trattoria was a local hangout. Business managers appeared, and tables filled quickly. The beautiful sound of Italian filled the small square as patrons began recounting stories of morning transactions, gesticulating wildly as they spoke.

Soon, the plate of steaming scallopini arrived. The velvety sauce exploded in Julian's mouth as he took the first bite. The risotto was creamy and rich and the local wine aromatic and light. The sensual air caressed his body. He could feel the tension lifting as he settled into the familiar and comforting pace of Roman life.

A few of the faces on the terrace glanced his direction. With creased foreheads, they looked as if they were trying to determine who he was. Had they seen him before? Was he Marcella's husband from America? What was he doing alone? That Angelo was showing him so much attention confirmed that he was someone important and, as lunch continued and wine flowed, the glances were less furtive and more protracted and obvious.

Rome was a big city made up of small neighborhoods. Marcella knew everyone in the historical center – particularly politicians, bankers, and lawyers. Her father had served in city government and had a lucrative legal consulting business. Marcella had a glowing and bright personality and, when they used to go out, her father's contemporaries always approached her and wanted to know of her latest adventures in America and invite her to social gatherings before she went back to the States. Julian, an introvert, was the faithful accompanying spouse who gave her moral support but remained, mostly, quiet and at the margins.

No one approached Julian despite their suspicions that he was Marcella's husband. Julian finished his lunch, ordered a cup of espresso, took another sip of wine, and then paid his tab. He took a leisure stroll toward the Pantheon, one of Marcella's favorite Roman monuments – an intact 2nd century structure that continued to be an architectural marvel – a single-cast cement dome open to the sky. He and Marcella had spent many an afternoon sitting in one of the cafes facing it, watching it change color as the sun set, and listening to a melodious accordion resonating off the walls of nearby buildings.

He had avoided walking past the Pantheon since his arrival. He fully expected that he would have broken down and sobbed uncontrollably, but, to his surprise, he felt peaceful and serene. It was here that he and Marcella married and where the city held a memorial for her father. He was sad and missed her, but he didn't feel despair or an inability to move forward with life. Perhaps during her long illness, he had already prepared for her passing.

Julian pressed on toward his apartment – their apartment – the one Marcella had inherited from her parents and they from Marcella's grandparents. He greeted another resident of the building, an older matronly woman, walking her white fluffy terrier along the perimeter of the excavations. They exchanged pleasantries before he climbed the marble staircase and entered the cavernous space.

It had always been full of life. When Marcella's parents were alive, there were weekly social gatherings and dinners for acquaintances and friends – a tight circle of venerable Roman families. Marcella was the only one who had married outside the caste, to an American who had humble puritan roots. The saving grace was that Julian was a classics scholar and had a facility for languages.

The space felt dark despite the large windows. Julian didn't see the point of turning on the many lamps. As he walked across the expansive room, he heard the echo of his steps reverberate off the plaster walls. He glanced inside a walnut-paneled study where Piero had worked. Julian had contemplated setting up his laptop on the desk there. He loved the smell of old books emanating from the tall cases carefully organized by subject, author, date, and size of binding. He settled, instead, for a small table near the center of the parlor. Camilla had carefully arranged a large sofa, several comfortable chaises, an expansive coffee table, and side tables with lamps on an oversize Persian carpet. Just to the right of that there was an antique Chinese table, lamp, and chair. As the summer heat increased, it made sense to be out in the open space where a pleasant breeze blew in from the windows.

He dropped an Italian journal on the table, turned on the lamp, and went into the kitchen to pour a glass of water. He returned, opened his computer, and checked emails that were just arriving from the States. His daughter, Luna, sent him an itinerary of her travels for later in the summer. She wondered if her dad was going to sell the apartment and, if so, whether she needed to book a hotel room.

Julian hadn't decided what to do about their home. It was worth a fortune and cost a fortune to maintain, but it had been in Marcella's family for generations, and Julian felt some obligation to preserve that legacy. His work and life were in Atlanta, and his daughters were still in college. It made little sense to keep it, but he wasn't quite ready to let it go, either.

Julian continued responding to emails. He reluctantly opened a folder on his computer with copies of a newly discovered Roman manuscript from the 4th century. He had agreed to translate it and write a commentary, but he was now feeling that he had taken on too much. What he really needed was a sabbatical, a change of pace, a time to recompose his life. He closed the computer, got up, laid down on the sofa to read the journal he had picked up and, before long, he had fallen asleep.

2

Chapter Two – First Glance

The next day, Julian approached the large windows of the main living area, pulled back the curtains, and opened them to the morning air. He retreated to the kitchen, poured a cup of coffee, and returned to take in the views. The sky was hazy yet clear, signaling another warm day. Traffic was already building, and a few lonely neighbors were out walking dogs at the edge of the park.

Julian had placed a large chaise and small table near the window so that he could read the papers, check email, and have breakfast, all while absorbing the enchanting views. He opened his laptop and clicked the link to a local online newspaper. He was fluent in Italian and able to skim the headlines. The Italian government faced another crisis as one party threatened to pull out of a fragile coalition. The US was holding another national election before which white nationalists were already sowing doubt about its integrity. He read with curiosity a feature article in the Italian press about the rising profile of Atlanta as a powerhouse of progressive politicians. He had grown up in the northeast but moved to Atlanta for an academic post in classics. He had grown to appreciate its natural beauty and the vibrant, diverse population that made the city welcoming for international businesses.

Julian glanced up from his laptop and noticed the artist from the day before walking along the edge of the archaeological park with his easel and canvas bag in hand. He stopped at the same spot under Julian's apartment and set up his materials. He opened the tripod legs of the easel, pulled out paints and palette, and set the partially completed canvas on the easel support.

The painter sat on the nearby bench, rolled up his sleeves, and tightened the laces on his shoes. He seemed more relaxed, leaning back on his arms and taking in the scene. He glanced back and forth between the canvas and the line of columns he had captured, contemplating the adjustments he would make to the painting.

He stood up, turned around to grab a bottle of water from his small bag, and looked up. He noticed Julian peering out of the window. Julian leaned back as if to retreat from sight, but not before catching the artist's eyes. They were dark, deep set, and alluring.

He got up from his chair, walked back into the main parlor, and prepared some papers for his work. The sensation of having seen the artist's eyes was like a flash of light that creates an impression on the retina and only, with time, disappears. As he sorted his papers, the furtive glance and eyes haunted him.

He showered and shaved. The apartment was laid out along the west-facing side of the building. The parlor and dining area faced Piazza Venezia. The kitchen was tucked away behind the dining area. The main entrance of the apartment was at the top of a broad marble staircase. On the right of the entrance, a hallway led to three sizable bedrooms, each with a pair of large windows overlooking the archaeological site.

Julian walked down the hallway to the second bedroom. It was where he and Marcella stayed when they were in Rome. He was used to its décor, the idiosyncrasies of the bathroom, and the sense of security it provided sandwiched between the master room farther down the hall and the small guestroom near the entry.

He opened the massive antique armoire. A couple of Marcella's dresses hung on the right. His summer clothes – jeans, slacks, and light shirts – hung on the left. He pulled out some underwear, socks, and a polo shirt from the drawers and carried them into the bathroom. He pulled off his tee-shirt and dropped his shorts on the marble floor.

He turned on the antique faucet and let the water run until it turned warm. He ran some over his face and spread some shaving cream on his cheeks. He was already tan from a few days on the beach near Savannah at the end of the semester. He was blessed with supple skin that aged well. He had a full head of wavy dark hair that had been cut short just before he left the States.

Julian had a lean runner's body with broad shoulders, firm pecs, taut abdomen, and a smooth chest. He ran the cold blade over his face, removing the white cream with each stroke. When he finished, he stepped over the edge of the deep tub, turned on the shower, and let the warm water run over his body. The silky verbena soap felt soothing on his skin.

After showering, he reached for a fluffy white cotton towel, dried himself and stepped into fresh undershorts and shorts and pulled the polo shirt over his head. He ran his fingers through his hair so that it would dry loosely, casually.

He walked back into the parlor, poured another cup of coffee, and walked toward the window. As he glanced out, the artist was busy tightening up the elements of the painting. He had several brushes set in a jar, each tipped in a different hue. Even from Julian's window, he could make out the brilliance of the colors and the striking way the setting had been composed on the canvas. He looked out over the archaeological site and marveled at what he saw. Even having sat in the window countless times before, he had never seen the angle of light, the contrast of shadows, the highlights on the columns, nor the character and movement of the trees as he was seeing them now. It was as if he had come upon a setting for the first time. He was stunned.

He sat at the window and continued to watch the artist make slight adjustments to the painting. The painter periodically stepped back and examined the piece, walking back up to it and making a minor stroke here and there.

A few tourists noticed his work and diverged from their trek toward the Colosseum, lingering behind him to take in the painting. He didn't seem annoyed. He chatted with several who made comments and asked questions. The artist stepped back so that his admirers could get closer and watch as he made small strokes here and there. He seemed unusually confident and generous in bringing people closer and closer into the work.

At one point, the painter turned to reach for a brush and sensed Julian observing from above. He paused, looked up, and nodded. Instead of retreating from view, Julian remained seated and nodded back. Again, the painter's eyes were penetrating and intense, something he imagined artists possessed, a natural asset for observation of detail and context. While the tourists continued to admire the canvas, the artist maintained his gaze at Julian.

Julian nodded again, now at the canvas, as if to show his approval. The artist grasped the message and smiled, tipping his hat slightly. He pivoted toward the painting and then contemplated the setting, taking a few steps back. With one arm stretched toward the canvas and the other curved toward the small group gathered near him, he waited for their verdict. "Is it finished?" he overheard him ask in English.

They all nodded. The artist then reached for a small brush to sketch his signature on the lower right side of the canvas. They applauded. He bowed.

The tourists walked on, and the artist packed his paints, brushes, and canvas. He sat on the stone bench, pulled out a pear, and bit into the soft fruit. He leaned back on his arms and let his head tilt back, taking in a few rays of sun that were spilling over the nearby buildings.

Julian retreated into the parlor space. He had an appointment with bankers, so he assembled the requisite papers and placed them in a leather shoulder bag. He walked out onto the street and made his way toward the bank. Julian glanced at the archaeological site and noticed the painter had already packed up and was walking across the Piazza Venezia.

The bank lobby looked like the inside of a Renaissance palace. Polychromatic marble covered the walls in geometric design. Bright light streamed from the windows high on the walls. He approached the reception desk and asked for Mr. Ferrucci.

"*Un attimo,*" the young lady said as she invited Julian to take a seat. She retreated into a series of offices in the back of the lobby. Shortly thereafter, an older gentleman dressed in a formal suit walked up to Julian, who stood to great him.

"*Mr. Ferrucci, piacere.*"

"Professor Phillips. It's always a pleasure. I'm sorry for the circumstances," he said in perfect English. "Come this way."

They walked down a hallway and into a traditional wood paneled office.

"*Un caffè?*"

"*No, grazie,*" Julian replied as he took a seat in front of Mr. Ferrucci's desk. Julian rubbed his hands nervously.

Ferrucci was probably in his sixties and well-groomed, already tan from a few days at the beach. He had thick, dark hair that had been carefully slicked back on his head. There was a hint of patchouli oil in the air. He opened a folder on the desk and reviewed several documents.

"Since you are Marcella's husband and recorded beneficiary, there's not much we need to do to give you access to the accounts. I presume you brought a death certificate."

Julian nodded, reaching into his briefcase to extract a document. He handed it to Ferrucci, who glanced at it and slid it under other papers in the folder.

"We'll need to update the signature cards. And you'll be happy to know we have electronic access to accounts. You can make deposits, transfer funds, and do other banking remotely – even from the States."

Julian relaxed a bit.

Ferrucci slid a spreadsheet to Julian's side of the desk. "Here's a list and record of Marcella's accounts."

Julian glanced at the document, his heart fluttering nervously. Blood raced to his forehead as he glanced at the figure at the bottom of the document, identifying the balance of her accounts. He was dumbfounded. Ferrucci must have noticed and said, "Yes. It's a lot."

"But I don't understand," Julian began. "Where did all of this come from?"

"As you know, Marcella's parents were well off. She was an only child and inherited their estate. The estate continued to grow dramatically from the investments Piero made. Except for the costs of maintaining the apartment, there are few other expenses."

"And I can withdraw funds?"

Ferrucci nodded and added, "There are limits to how much you can take out of the country at a time. But yes, you can withdraw funds. Can you sign here?" Ferrucci asked, sliding another form to Julian.

Julian made a few signatures, and Ferrucci made copies. They stood in front of Ferrucci's desk and shook hands. "Thank you," Julian said.

"I was a childhood friend of Piero's, and I have known the family for decades. It has always been an honor to work with Marcella and her parents. I am saddened by her death. I hope I will have the honor of continuing to work with you."

"I don't see why anything would change. You've been a devoted and loyal friend."

Ferrucci smiled warmly and held the back of Julian's arm as he walked with him toward the door.

Julian left Ferrucci's office, walked out into the lobby and then into the bright midday sunlight. While Julian knew Marcella's parents had set up a trust, and he had known a few of the details, he was ignorant of the full magnitude of his wife's wealth. He was overwhelmed.

Disoriented, he wandered aimlessly through the maze of streets in the historical center of Rome. He came upon the Piazza Navona and strolled past Bernini's Four Rivers fountain. He chuckled at the assortment of artists set up on the square selling watercolors to tourists. He remarked how different their work was from the artist under his window. Did he have a studio? Where did he sell his work? Should he buy something to remind him of a setting he was likely to relinquish if he sold the apartment?

He returned home, stopping first at the edge of the archaeological park. He sat on the same stone bench the artist had used earlier in the day, absorbing the perspective that had inspired him, trying to sense what he must have sensed to produce such a compelling image.

The sun had traveled further west, filtering through the umbrella pines on the far side of the excavations. An afternoon breeze from the sea cooled the air. He glanced toward Trajan's column covered in detailed carvings of the emperor's exploits and Rome's heritage. Although he studied ancient Roman texts, he always felt as if he were an observer looking at another age and place. For a brief moment, sitting calmly at the edge of Roman ruins under the windows of his Roman apartment, he felt like he might belong. It was ironic, given that all personal connections to Rome were now departed. Why, suddenly, did he sense he was at home?

3

Chapter Three – The Card

The next morning, Julian woke early. He had a disturbing dream and couldn't fall back to sleep. He made some coffee, fixed some breakfast, and read early editions of the day's electronic papers on a sofa in the parlor.

Between articles, he tried to piece together the elusive elements of the dream. He felt as if he were racing toward something, trying to grab hold of it, and it kept receding from reach. The images were blurred, but the emotions were strong – a sense of dissonance and the desperate hope that if he could just grab hold of this thing running from him, he could feel whole again.

He showered and shaved and, when he went into the bedroom to get some clothes, he noticed Marcella's dresses again. "It's time," he said out loud to himself. He took hold of the hangers, folded the dresses loosely, and carried them into the kitchen. He found a shopping bag, placed them inside, and decided to donate them to a local charity run at a nearby parish.

He had an appointment with a scholar at the Capitoline Museums that morning. He walked outside the apartment and made his way across the Piazza Venezia and toward the ramp that led up to the museums and the charming square designed by Michelangelo. He climbed the ramp, gazed at the towering statues of Castor and Pollux, and made his way to the security entrance of the museum.

He presented his credentials, and the attendant waved him inside, making a call to a certain Professoressa Luciana Alfano. In a few minutes, a woman appeared in the reception area.

"Julian," she said warmly as she extended her hands to greet him.

"Luciana," he replied enthusiastically, giving her a kiss on both cheeks.

"I'm so sorry to hear about Marcella," she added, placing her hand affectionately on his forearm.

"*Grazie,*" he said. "*Mi manca.*"

"I imagine you do miss her. She was such a dear."

Luciana was roughly Julian's age. Her blue skirt, white blouse, and gray jacket reinforced her academic identity even though Julian knew she partied hard. Her hair had grayed considerably over the last year, and she now wore it pulled back. He gazed into her piercing green eyes. "So, what is new with you?"

"Nothing much. I work. I play. I repeat."

"And you haven't settled down?"

Luciana paused and said, "Not really."

"What does that mean?" he asked, raising one of his brows.

"I'm seeing someone, but I like my freedom and independence. You were lucky with Marcella. You both seemed to have had a nice balance between your professional lives and your time together."

"You're a catch," Julian said excitedly. "I'm sure there are all kinds of guys interested."

Luciana stared at Julian. Her green eyes lingered just long enough to make him uncomfortable. He always wondered if she had been interested in him. It was curious that just after Marcella died, she contacted him about a recently discovered manuscript from Ostia that needed translation and commentary.

"Let's go to the archives. I want you to see the original manuscript."

They walked through some of the galleries of one of the oldest museums in Europe. It contained some of the most important ancient Roman artifacts, and it was an important center for new research and archaeological discoveries. Julian breathed in the air of the revered space. As a classicist, the pieces he passed were familiar to him, as if they were friends and acquaintances. He knew their origins, their journeys from one location or museum to another, and their imprint on history. He found it difficult to comprehend Luciana passing nonchalantly past them, as if they were little more than molding or decoration. They descended to a corridor connecting the two main buildings of the museum under the main office of the City of Rome. Excavations had been done on the Tabularium. They walked through soaring arches where manuscripts and scrolls had been preserved during the height of the Roman empire.

They entered an air-conditioned area and passed into a hermetically controlled room. "*Ecco!*" she exclaimed as she pointed to the manuscript. "It's amazing that it was found and so well preserved."

Julian peered at the ancient codex. It was a small book or journal written on parchment. Many of the documents he had seen and studied before were papyrus scrolls or individual sheets of parchment.

"And what is it again?" Julian asked, already knowing the answer but easing into a more protracted professional conversation.

"It's the personal reflections of a 4th century business owner from Ostia."

"And it's importance?"

"That's for you to determine and write about."

"Can you give me a few clues?" he pressed Luciana.

"Well, from what we can determine, the author's wife was a Christian and a deaconess. The reflections appear to be an attempt to identify what he finds appealing about Christianity while still expressing reticence."

Julian's eyes widened as he gazed at the manuscript. He beamed and nodded. "I'm eager to begin work. This might be an interesting insight into the transition from pagan traditions to Christian ones."

"That's what everyone suspects. Are you going to work on it here in Rome or back in Atlanta?"

"I thought I would spend a little time here, settling Marcella's estate and enjoying time away from campus."

Julian couldn't help noticing Luciana's delight at the news – a delight she tried to hide behind professional collegiality. "If you want to come back here and look at the original or if you'd like to get together to discuss your findings, I'm always happy to oblige."

"I wouldn't want to take you from your work or intrude upon your summer plans."

Luciana waved her hands dismissively. "It would be a pleasure to spend time with you."

Julian smiled, turning evasively toward the manuscript. He examined it without touching the parchment, and he and Luciana discussed the circumstances within which it was discovered, new archaeological work at Ostia Antica, and news about the Capitoline Museums.

After a while, Julian glanced at his watch. "Thanks for showing me this," he said. "I realize I have another appointment across town in a short while."

"Don't let me hold you back," she replied, closing the protective cover of the codex and leading them back out into the office area. "Why don't we have dinner sometime," she said.

"That would be nice. I'll call you."

They embraced. Luciana said, "You know your way out?"

"Yes. Thanks. *Ci vediamo.*"

"*Ciao,*" she said warmly.

Julian walked out of the museum into the shaded piazza. He didn't have an appointment but wasn't ready to engage with Luciana more. He strolled over to a driveway that led to an overlook of the Forum on the western side of the Roman archives. This was one of the most iconic views of the Forum, looking out over the broad expanse of the archaeological site with the columns of the temple of the Dioscuri - Castor and Pollux - floating in the middle of the park, the temple of Antonino and Faustina in the distance, the small white marble remnants of the temple of Vesta in the center, the Arch of Titus in the far distance and, beyond that, the massive arches of the Colosseum.

To Julian's surprise, the artist who had been painting below his window was painting on the edge of the terrace, capturing the late morning light as it bathed the Forum. A heavy haze accentuated shafts of light that pierced the graceful columns filtering through a few solitary umbrella pines perched high on the Palatine Hill.

A crowd of tourists leaned against the railing, taking pictures of the scene. A few stood behind the artist, watching as he sketched the setting on canvas. Julian joined those behind the artist and watched as he brought the elements of the scene together.

The artist turned to retrieve a brush behind him and caught Julian's eye. Julian recoiled spontaneously, as if he had been caught trespassing. The artist acknowledged Julian and smiled. He turned back to the canvas and began blocking in some of the darker sections of the landscape – the brick foundations of ancient structures and the vegetation clinging to the slopes of the Palatine.

Julian noticed the artist had a small container attached to his easel filled with business cards. The next time to painter pivoted toward him, Julian reached toward the case and asked, "*Posso?*"

The artist nodded, dipping another brush into a mixture of yellow paint as he blocked in the bright sky. He faced the canvas and began placing squiggly lines of yellow next to irregular lines of turquoise and blue. Julian gazed at the artist's card. It was simple, with a light impression of the forum in the background and dark lettering in the foreground. *Bruno Muzzi. Artista. Olio su tela.* On the reverse side were a phone number and website.

Julian watched Bruno bring the scene to life on his canvas. Periodically, he stepped back from the canvas and contemplated the setting – feeling the values or intensity of light and sensing the shape and form of the structures in the composition. The artist furrowed his brows and squinted his eyes as he alternated between focus and a more diffused impression. Engrossed in the process, the artist was oblivious to his surroundings and the tourists watching him paint.

He pivoted toward his canvas bag to reach for a bottle of water. He nodded to those standing behind him and, as he took a long sip, he caught Julian's eye again and lingered. Julian felt the intensity of Bruno's gaze and wanted to look evasively away, but found Bruno's eyes difficult to resist. He let himself look back, his own hazel eyes scrutinizing Bruno's. Bruno placed the bottle back in the bag and turned toward the canvas, moving a brush loaded with dark pigment across the lower part of the painting. He set that brush in a jar, reached for another, dipped it in a mixture of turquoise, rose, and blue that formed an intense purple color and made a few crucial strokes to highlight shadows. Suddenly, the elements of the painting leaped out into three dimensions. Bruno smiled and turned toward Julian, not concealing the intent to solicit his reaction.

Julian stood out in the crowd. He was alone, tall, and handsome – and he didn't look like a tourist. Even in his casual but professional clothes, Bruno noticed Julian's athletic body. His shoulders were broad, the upper sleeves of his shirt bulged slightly around biceps, and he had raised one of his legs onto the brick embankment, his thighs pressing firmly against the fabric of his slacks.

He had only briefly noticed him the day before and wondered if he was a business executive, a diplomat, or perhaps a stray tourist. Whatever, Bruno was intrigued and hoped his admirer might be more forward and introduce himself.

Julian placed his elbow on the upper part of his leg and rested his chin on the back of his hand, showing he was in no hurry and intended to observe the artist for a protracted period. Bruno seemed delighted at the attention and, with a big grin, turned back to the canvas to work.

Bruno was working in full sun and had a small umbrella attached to his easel to shade the canvas. He wore a broad-brimmed straw hat, a long-sleeve sheer linen shirt, and shorts. A light breeze occasionally lifted the tails of his shirt, exposing a dark hairy torso. Bruno had a thin waist. His shorts hung loosely on his hips. He had muscular and dark hairy legs and wore stylish soft leather sneakers.

Julian chuckled to himself at how atypical Bruno was from other artists he had seen before. He was unusually handsome and well-groomed. This seemed to carry over to his materials. His easel was spotless, and he used a freshly cleaned palette for each session. His brushes were organized and, when he finished a session, they were wrapped in a fresh rag. There were no paint marks on his shirt or shorts.

Bruno was graceful in his strokes and oscillated back and forth between canvas, palette, and brushes. He was engrossed in the process of painting, but took time to stretch, do a few squats, and twist his upper torso to keep from getting stiff.

Groups of tourists passed by, snapping photos of the forum and lingering behind Bruno to observe his work. Julian remained, savoring the breeze on the edge of the terrace and contemplating the setting, which he never tired of. There were always extra details to notice in the archaeological park – a tumbled capital or a solitary piece of marble secured to an ancient wall or the remnant of a frieze or plaque.

Bruno continued to tighten the composition on the canvas, using tighter and tighter brushes as the painting progressed. He was cognizant of Julian's presence and became less furtive in his glances and more relaxed, as if Julian were not just a passing tourist but someone familiar, perhaps someone to keep him company as he worked.

Julian eventually felt the intensity of the midday sun and decided to head home. The next time Bruno glanced his way, he tapped his watch, nodded, and then retreated. Bruno nodded and waved at him with a brush.

Back home, Julian looked up Bruno's website. He was a native Roman who specialized in original oil paintings of ancient Roman sites. He had won several awards at local juried shows and was represented by several prestigious galleries in Rome, Milan, and Paris. The website had several sample images of his work, but little else in terms of photos, contact information, or other details about Bruno's life.

Julian took a walk after lunch and went to Via Margutta, where one of the galleries showed Bruno's paintings. The narrow road just below the Borghese Park and the Pincio Hill was lined with exclusive shops, including several art dealers. Julian located the gallery noted on Bruno's website and went inside. A slender, stylish woman looked up from her desk and welcomed him in English.

"Do you have any works by Bruno Muzzi?" Julian asked.

The clerk stood up, nodded, and led Julian to a wall where several stunning images of the Colosseum and Constantine's Arch were on display under bright studio lights. "These are two we have left of his last show. He's working on a new series, and we hope to have another exhibit in September. Are you familiar with his work?"

"I came across him working and looked him up. I'm embarrassed to say I wasn't familiar with him before."

"Are you from the States?"

Julian nodded.

"Bruno is better known by local collectors. By the way, my name is Gabriella."

"*Piacere*," Julian said, extending his hand in a shake.

"*Lei parla Italiano?*"

"*Sì, un po'.*"

"How is it you speak Italian?" Gabriella pressed Julian, her eyes widening at the prospect of a more extended exchange.

"I've spent some time here over the years," Julian replied, concealing his deeper connections.

Julian looked intently at Bruno's work, sensing Gabriella's gaze and scrutiny. She was obviously trying to ascertain whether he was a collector or just a casual tourist. Julian walked closer to one of the pieces and furrowed his brow, looking closely at the brush strokes and blended colors. "His work is amazing," Julian murmured.

Gabriella nodded and approached Julian. As she got closer, he breathed in her scent. It was familiar to him - Marcella's. There was something peculiar in the Roman air that created a unique mix of smells – earthy, citrusy, sweet. Julian loved the elegance of Roman women, their stylish boots, short skirts, scarves, and artistic glasses that often complemented the color of their hair.

"You mentioned there would be a show in September. Can I get on a list so that you can notify me?"

Gabriella nodded and walked to her desk, opened the computer, and pulled up a contact list. "Your name?"

"Julian Phillips."

Gabriella looked up and her eyes widened. "You're not related to Marcella, are you?"

"She's my wife - or I should say, my late wife."

Gabriella raised her hand to her mouth. "Oh my God. Did she pass?"

Julian nodded, holding back emotions.

"How?"

"Breast cancer."

"I'm so sorry. We were classmates in school. We lost touch over the years, but I saw news about her parents passing and noticed she had married an American."

"That's me."

Gabriella stood up, approached Julian, and gave him a warm embrace. "*Mi dispiace*," she said, wiping a few tears off her cheeks as she expressed her grief.

"*Grazie*," he said back.

"So, what do you do?"

"I'm a classics professor."

"That's not surprising given Marcella's father's interests."

"Yes. I think it helped him get over the fact that Marcella was marrying an American – outside of the Roman clan."

Gabriella let out a light chuckle and then, more seriously, asked, "So, was it a long illness?

Julian nodded, choking back tears. Gabriella placed her hand on his forearm tenderly.

"What did Marcella do in the States?"

"She was a philanthropist."

"That suits her personality."

"She was very good at raising money for good causes. You know how social she was."

Gabriella nodded. "Did you spend a lot of time here?"

"We joined Piero and Camilla for vacations in the summer and usually came at Christmas. That was about it. It was difficult for me to get away from school much more than that. And we had two girls."

"Ah. I assume they are grown?"

"They're in college."

"Did Marcella inherit her parents' home?"

"Yes. Her parents had inherited it from her grandparents and when they passed, it became ours. I'm trying to figure that out now."

"That must be so difficult. If you need anything, let me know. By the way, I think Marcella's father might have a few of Bruno's pieces."

"Hmm. I never noticed. But I just became acquainted with his work. I'll have to look."

Gabriella handed Julian her card. "Here's my contact information if you ever want to be in touch."

"Here's mine," he said in reply, handing her his card. "Please put me in the contact list so you can alert me to Bruno's next show."

"Certainly."

There was an awkward silence and then Julian said, "It was a pleasure to meet you. I'm sure we will be in touch."

"I hope so," Gabriella said warmly, giving Julian a kiss on his cheeks.

Julian strolled back to Piazza Venezia along the Via Del Corso. He climbed the stairs to the apartment and went inside, turning on all the lamps to examine Piero's collection of paintings. Sure enough, on the wall near the dining area, there were two paired paintings of the Via Appia Antica done by Bruno. They framed a large antique sideboard. One included a few broken tombs under the shade of cypress and pine trees; the other a scene of the road near an ancient aqueduct. Julian turned on the light over the dining table and walked up close to the paintings. They were clearly Bruno's style – loose brush strokes, contrasting light, and intriguing composition – a scene that invited one in.

As he gazed at the painting of the aqueduct, an impression of Bruno floated through the air – his powerful forearm stretched toward the canvas and his face concentrating on the careful placement of a few strokes of light hue for the arched structure. He could sense Bruno's concentration and thoughtfulness. Bruno didn't just see the setting and replicate it. He felt the setting – its warmth, movement, and energy – and conveyed that feeling in strokes that alternated between tender caresses and playful dabs. The serenity of the Via Appia was evident in the composition. It was meditative and ethereal. He wondered if the warmth and pensive quality of the painting reflected Bruno's personality or if he channeled the mood of a location.

He went into the kitchen and cut a few pieces of cheese and prosciutto and poured a glass of wine, returning to the parlor where he sat in one of the large chaises. He sat back in the chair, took a sip of wine, and ruminated on the day. Bruno's notoriety surprised him. It was also interesting to meet someone outside of Piero's and Camilla's circle who knew Marcella. The fact that Gabriella was her classmate was remarkable.

Meeting Luciana at the Capitoline Museum and Gabriella at the gallery underscored a dilemma for Julian. How involved did he want to remain with people in Rome? Marcella's extended family had never embraced Julian enthusiastically. After her parents passed, their trips to Rome were less frequent and usually involved some formal event Marcella had to attend or some business matter she had to take care of. Julian would accompany her, but spent his time doing research or attending a conference. Their real friends and social life were in the States.

Julian had a meeting the next day with lawyers to discuss the details of the rest of the estate, particularly the residence. He eased back in the chair, pulled out his iPad, and began to read a novel he had been wanting to tackle. He woke later, realizing he had dozed off. He went back into the bedroom, crawled into bed, and fell into a sound sleep.

4

Chapter Four – The Estate

Julian woke, ate a light breakfast, showered, and dressed for his meeting with lawyers. He slipped several documents, including a Marcella's death certificate, into a briefcase and walked toward the Prati area of Rome. He located the address of the law firm that handled Piero's estate, rang the bell on the outside intercom, and was promptly buzzed in. He climbed two sets of stairs and entered an upscale office. A receptionist greeted him.

"You must be Julian Phillips. I'm Sonia. You are here to see to see Mr. Alberti and Mr. Caruso, correct?"

Julian nodded.

"They will be with you shortly. Would you like coffee or water?"

"No thanks," Julian said, taking a seat in the reception area.

A few moments later, an older gentleman walked into the area. Julian stood and shook his hands.

"*Professor Phillips, benvenuto,*" Mr. Alberti said warmly. "I'm sorry for your loss."

Julian nodded as Mr. Alberti led him down the hall to a large office. "Julian, this is Mr. Caruso. Roberto, this is Professor Phillips."

"*Piacere.*"

"Have a seat," Alberti said. He sat down at the desk with Caruso sitting to the side. He opened files. "I believe you have already been to the bank to settle the trust funds. What we need to do today is formalize your status as Marcella's survivor and beneficiary of the trust associated with the residence."

Julian nodded anxiously.

Caruso began, "There are a lot of unique laws in Italy and in Rome that govern transactions regarding real estate, particularly real estate in a historical district and adjacent to national patrimonial sites such as the Forum."

"What does that mean in this case?" Julian inquired.

"Although Marcella was the only child of Piero and Camilla, the real estate trust has been in the family for generations. There are provisions in the trust that forbid selling the property outside the family."

Julian looked perplexed.

Alberti continued, "You inherit the residence, but you can't sell it outside of the family."

"Who is the family?"

Caruso replied, "Piero's brothers had children. They are the next in line if you and your children pass or if you or your children decide to sell the residence. They would have the right of first refusal. Then the option goes to relations that are more distant. If no one wants to buy the residence, and you still insist on selling it, it must be offered to the Comune di Roma per Piero's great-great-grandfather's stipulations.

"Ah," Julian murmured, rubbing his chin thoughtfully.

"Have you given any thought to your plans?" Caruso inquired.

"Not yet. I am still trying to get over Marcella's passing and have been involved in end of semester responsibilities in Atlanta. I just arrived the other day, and I'm trying to piece together information about the estate."

"I'm sure it's a painful time and complicated process. Take your time. There's no urgency to make a decision," Alberti underscored. "We need you to sign a few documents here. We are at your disposal should you wish to sell the residence or if you need to file any documentation with the government."

"I have a question," Julian tentatively began, clearing his throat.

Alberti and Caruso nodded and leaned forward.

"Are there any of Piero's nephews or nieces that have expressed interest in the residence?"

Alberti and Caruso looked at each other. Caruso began, "Yes. One of his nieces is very interested. She's actually begun inquiries about your status."

"Is she contesting the will?" Julian asked with a bit of alarm.

"Not yet," Alberti noted, raising his brows.

"What does that mean? Does she have any grounds to contest it?"

"We don't think so," Caruso added. "But she could set in motion a series of legal maneuvers that would create a lot of problems and be expensive to fight."

Julian settled back into his chair and rubbed his chin again. "Can I count on your support? Do you have any conflicts of interest?"

Alberti and Caruso looked at each other and Caruso began, "Yes, you can count on us. We don't represent anyone in the family except you."

Julian breathed a sigh of relief.

Alberti slid some documents toward Julian for his signature. Julian signed them.

"Any other questions?" Caruso asked.

"Are there other requirements or provisions associated with the residence that I need to be concerned with?"

Alberti replied, "There are city limitations on renovations and requirements about upkeep. As you probably suspect, it is an expensive building to maintain."

"Any suggestions?" Julian asked.

"The association of owners probably has a professional manager. You might want to engage someone to look after your unit – making sure there are no issues when you are away. We have some companies that we can recommend."

"I would be very appreciative," Julian said, rising as if to show he was ready to leave.

Alberti and Caruso rose, shook his hands, and said, "Again, we are sorry for your loss. Piero and Camilla were close friends, and we always loved seeing Marcella. She was a delight. She was so talented."

Julian nodded and then turned, walking out into the reception area, down the staircase, and out into the sunlight.

The weight of responsibility for the residence felt heavy, and Julian wondered what he should do. It would be easier to sell it to the niece than having to maintain it and fend off legal challenges. But there was a little voice in the back of his head, one that sounded a lot like Marcella's, saying, "*Piano, piano*. Take it slowly. There's no need to rush to a decision."

Julian walked across town and decided to climb the Capitoline Hill to see if Bruno was painting. He was eager to introduce himself and share information about the gallery he visited and the pieces his father-in-law had in his apartment.

He walked along the old medieval streets leading from the Prati neighborhood to the Campo de' Fiori. He strolled through the busy market, taking in the ripe smells of fresh vegetables and fruit. He bought a pear and bit into it, some of the warm juice running down his arm. He stopped in a small café and asked for some mineral water and a coffee and continued toward the Capitoline Hill.

On the terrace overlooking the Forum, he searched for Bruno.

There were scores of tourists pressed against the railing taking self-ies, photos, and waving off aggressive vendors. There was another artist who had set up a rack of watercolors, but Bruno was nowhere to be found. Julian looked to the other terrace and along some of the side roads to see if Bruno had set up in another area, but he saw no one.

As he stood looking out over the Forum, he got a text from Luciana. "*Ciao*, Julian. I'm having a few people over to my place this evening. Are you free? It would be great if you could come?"

Julian murmured to himself, "That was quick." He wasn't sure he wanted to play into what he presumed was Luciana's curiosity and interest in him, but he had nothing else to do and thought it might be nice to meet some people and get out of the apartment.

"Sure. When and where?"

She gave him a time and address just off the Via Giulia.

Later that evening, Julian stepped out of his residence and walked toward Luciana's apartment. He crossed the Piazza Venezia and strolled toward the Largo Argentina, an expansive excavated square with ancient Roman temples. He peered down at the foundations which dated back to the 3rd and 2nd centuries BCE. He marveled at a few columns that were illuminated by the golden light of sunset and thought of Bruno and how he might paint such a scene.

He continued toward the Campo de' Fiori, the open-air market that, in the evening, was transformed into a piazza filled with cafes. Off the square were a series of small lanes which led into 15th and 16th century neighborhoods that had become fashionable and pricey. He and everyone else loved the timelessness of the zone – the ochre-stained walls, antique streetlights, broad beamed eaves, and small cozy restaurants tucked away here and there.

He found Luciana's address, pressed the intercom, and she buzzed him up. He climbed the stairs to the upper-level unit and pressed the door open. She had an expansive residence with tall, dark-stained wood beam ceilings, antique red tile floor, and large stone windows overlooking the street.

"Julian, *benvenuto!*" Luciana approached him and gave him kisses on both cheeks. She grabbed hold of his upper arm and led him into the center of the room. "I want to introduce you to some friends."

"*Stefano, voglio presentarti Julian. Julian, Stefano,*" Luciana said as she approached a tall 40-year-old man who was strikingly handsome – broad shouldered, tall angular face, a full head of dark hair, and a trim light beard lining his prominent jaw and circling his mouth.

He extended his hand to Julian, "*Piacere.*"

As Luciana dragged him farther into the room, Julian felt Stefano's lingering gaze. "*Luca, Julian. Julian, questo è Luca, un mio collega al museo.*" She continued in English, "Julian is working with the new Ostia codex.

"Oh! You're the Julian Luciana has been talking about! Nice to meet you. We are looking forward to your work," Luca added in perfect English.

"What would you like to drink," Luciana asked Julian.

"*Vino rosso se c'è.*"

"*Un attimo,*" Luciana said as she retreated to the kitchen to get some wine. She left Luca and Julian talking. Several other people in the room glanced Julian's way. A woman walked toward him.

"You must be Julian. I'm Sofia. *Piacere,*" Sofia said as she extended her hand to him. Almost as if posing as a model, her body faced Luca, but her head faced Julian. She had piercing blue eyes and short blond hair resting playfully on her long, beautiful neck. She wore a single piece tight black dress. Julian couldn't help noticing her heeled sandals and turquoise painted toenails.

"Julian. *Piacere.*"

Luca said, "Oh. *Scusate.* You haven't met?"

Julian nodded no.

Luca looked toward the kitchen and noticed Luciana approaching them. He paused. Luciana handed Julian a glass of wine and put her hand affectionately on Sofia's shoulder. "I see you just met."

Julian nodded.

"Sofia is my partner."

"Your partner at the museum?" Julian asked.

"No, my life partner."

Surprised, Julian struggled to find an appropriate segue. "*Auguri,*" was all he managed to get out.

"Thank you," Luciana said, staring at Julian as if to read his reaction. "We've been seeing each other for a while," she said as she peered into Sofia's eyes and pursed her lips in an air kiss.

Julian looked inquisitively at Luciana and then at Sofia and said, "Are you from Rome?"

She nodded. "I grew up here. I went away for studies and work, but I have recently returned. I understand your late wife was from here."

"Yes. We used to come often. In recent years, not so much. It's been nice to catch up with Luciana. It's nice to meet you."

"My pleasure. Nice to meet you, and I'm sure we'll have more time to chat later."

Luciana grabbed his hand and dragged him over to a couple of men. She evaded Julian's scrutinizing look.

"*Franco e Roberto, Juilian. Un amico dagli Stati Uniti.* Julian – these are my dear friends Franco and Roberto. They live around the corner. Franco is a professor at the University of Rome, and Roberto is an architect."

"*Piacere,*" Julian replied. He was finding it difficult to keep track of everyone's name and their varying relationships. Franco was quirky looking - tall, lean, fair complexion, tousled hair, and an oversized nose. It was easy to place him at the front of a classroom. Roberto looked just like an architect or an artist – with a more substantial physical frame, long wavy hair, hazel eyes, high cheeks, and a late-day shadow lining his jaw and circling his mouth. He wore a stylish high-collar sweater and fashionable jeans. He smiled warmly over the top of his glass of wine.

"What do you teach?" Julian asked Franco.

"Classical history. I understand you're a classics scholar yourself."

Julian smiled. "I assume Luciana has told you of my new work with the codex from Ostia."

"Yes. It is very exciting. Hopefully, you will spend some time in Rome. We'd love to have you over some time."

"That would be nice," Julian replied, giving each a protracted look.

He continued chatting with Roberto and Franco and then saw Luciana leave a small group of people and head toward the kitchen. Julian excused himself and pursued her quickly.

She saw him enter the kitchen and grinned sheepishly. Julian asked, "Well?"

"Well, what?" she replied evasively.

"Spill."

"She's nice, isn't she?" Luciana interjected, avoiding the question that was lying on the table.

"When did you begin seeing women?" Julian pressed her further.

"I don't know. It just happened. It was a surprise."

"No clues or signals in advance?"

"In retrospect, maybe. I never really connected with any one guy. I had fun, but at some level, things never clicked. Sofia and I met at a party. We had a great conversation, and we continued it afterward at a bar. She was very flirtatious and affectionate. I liked it. We met again for dinner and went back to her place. I had never been with a woman, but it felt natural. I never looked back."

"Good for you!" Julian exclaimed.

"And you?" Luciana asked. "I know it is early after Marcella's death, but do you see yourself dating?"

"I haven't given it a lot of thought, yet. However, since Marcella was so sick for the last year, I feel like I have been mourning her loss for a while. It's odd. When she passed, it was a relief. I'm ready to get on with my life."

"I'm sure you are. That's why I asked you to translate and write a commentary on the new codex. I was hoping it would provide you an opportunity to get out of your house and do some new things and meet new people."

"You're not trying to set me up, are you – with Luca or someone like that?"

Luciana grinned. She looked off to avert Julian's eyes and said, "No. But I have a lot of friends who I would like you to meet and who I think would find you quite interesting and attractive."

"Men or women?"

"Does it matter?"

Julian paused and considered the question. He would have instinctively answered yes. It mattered. He was interested in women. But the question intrigued him, and Luciana's new self-awareness gave him reason to ponder his own circumstances. Nevertheless, he responded promptly, "Women."

Luciana smiled as if to say, 'we'll see.' "Can you help me bring this tray into the living room?" she asked as she headed toward the parlor.

Julian reached for the tray and carried it into the parlor, setting it down on a low table near the sofa. He stood back up and took a sip of his wine. He looked around the room and realized he might be the only straight person in the crowd. Oddly, he felt very much at home. He wasn't sure if it was because he was back in Rome, which always felt like home to him, or whether it was that he was back in Rome socializing with people who were more his age and had similar interests to his than Marcella's parents and their friends. Rome felt tribal to him, and through Marcella, he had been let into a select group of venerable Romans. He spoke Italian like a native, acquired Roman mannerisms, and circulated comfortably and nimbly amongst the Roman elite.

He observed Luciana's friends – a coterie of scholars, artists, and curators. They were a different tribe. Privileged, yes. But they were the *avant-garde* of culture, the ones who brought to the surface new perspectives. Julian felt more of an affinity with them and wanted to belong. As he scanned the crowd, he caught Stefano staring at him from the other side of the room. They smiled at each other. Julian murmured to himself, "Well, at least I'm not an invisible old man." He took a sip of wine and grinned sheepishly from behind the glass. He wondered if he hadn't found a new tribe.

5

Chapter Five – Runner

Julian rose the next morning and decided to take a run. It had been a while since he had been able to exercise, and he was ready to get back into a routine. He pulled on his shorts, slipped on a lightweight shirt, and tightened the laces of his running shoes. He did some stretches on the carpet in the parlor and then headed down the stairs and out into the fresh morning air.

He had a favorite route he and Marcella had run years before and headed down the Via dei Fori Imperiali toward the main entrance to the Roman Forum. He was grateful for the generous cushions of his shoes, as the cobblestone pavement was hard. He ran along the outer wall of the Basilica of Maxentius, the soaring brick arches of one of the larger ruins of the Forum. As he approached the Colosseum and the pedestrian zone nearby, he turned right past the Arch of Constantine and under the shade of umbrella pines along the roadway hugging the lower slopes of the Palatine Hill.

He was out of shape and could feel his lungs struggle to get enough oxygen to sustain the pace he had set. He turned right at the Circus Maximus and, climbing the incline on the east side of the large open space, his upper legs began to burn. At the top of the hill, he decided to slow to a fast walk, and continued down the hill toward Santa Maria in Cosmedin and the nearby Forum Boarium. A pleasant breeze kicked in, and Julian felt a renewed rush of energy course through his body. He decided to extend his run under the shaded road hugging the Tiber River.

He paused for a break in the grassy park surrounding the ancient temple of Hercules in what had been a marketplace in ancient Rome where boats riding up from Ostia unloaded their goods. The temple was the oldest preserved temple made of marble from ancient Rome, dating back to the 2nd century BCE. It was circular, with graceful, fluted marble columns and an inner arched chamber that supported a tile roof. Julian stretched and was about to head up the hill to the roadway along the river when he spotted a painter on the other side of the park.

He arched his head around the monument and watched the artist unfold his easel. When the artist turned to set a canvas bag down on the grass, he noticed it was Bruno. Julian watched him level the easel on the ground and then squeeze paint onto the palette. As Julian got closer, Bruno looked up and cast a smile of recognition. Julian waved back.

Bruno continued to unpack supplies and arrange things for his session. Once he had propped the canvas on the easel, he focused on the setting, squinting his eyes at the structure and stepping back to feel the play of light and shadow. He squeezed out a little dark gray paint and dipped a brush in it. He extended his arm toward the canvas and, while looking at the temple, made a few tentative strokes to form the outline of the monument. He glanced back at Julian briefly and then pivoted toward the canvas.

He reached for another brush and dipped it in a lighter hue and make a few strokes that formed the perimeter of the columns that were directly in the light. He continued sketching out the roof, the underside of the roof, the base of the temple, and then the columns that were shaded. Julian could see how the scene began to take shape and form on the canvas and smiled in admiration.

Bruno looked at him and waved him forward. Julian approached and said, "*Non voglio disturbarvi.*"

"*Non è un disturbo,*" Bruno said, assuring Julian that he wasn't bothering him.

"*Sono Julian.*"

"*Piacere. Bruno.*"

Julian nodded for Bruno to continue. Bruno turned toward the easel, mixed a few paints to create other hues, and added color and detail to the painting. It rapidly took shape. Bruno looked back at Julian, who looked at the painting and nodded a warm, approving smile.

"*È bellissimo. Mi piace molto!*" he said to Bruno, conveying how much he liked it.

"*Lei è Americano?*" Bruno asked, wondering if Julian wasn't American.

Julian nodded.

"Your Italian is very good, but I detect a slight accent."

"I've tried to overcome it," Julian said, grinning.

Bruno turned back toward the canvas and continued to work.

Julian casually interjected as Bruno continued to move back and forth between the palette and the canvas, "I noticed you the other day at Trajan's Forum and then again at The Roman Forum. Do you paint primarily Roman scenes?"

"Exclusively archaeological sites."

Julian gazed back at Bruno with curiosity. "I discovered your work at the gallery on Via Margutta."

"Did you speak with Gabriella? *È carina, no?*"

"Yes. She's very nice. Very beautiful. She mentioned a show in September."

"Yes. As you can see, I'm trying to get a lot done."

"Don't let me take you from your work."

"I don't mind as long as you don't mind if I work."

Julian nodded no. He asked, "Why Roman archaeology?"

"Layers."

Bruno squeezed some cobalt blue, white, and some other hues Julian couldn't identify on the palette. He mixed them and applied the paint to the sky. Julian's eyes lit up as the temple became even more pronounced.

"What do you mean, layers?"

"History, epochs, texture, light, and dark. It's like life. There's so much hidden or unnoticed. I like to bring out small architectural elements that were part of a story but are often overlooked."

Julian smiled.

Bruno asked, "Are you on vacation?"

"Business."

"What do you do?"

"I'm a professor of classical history."

Bruno paused, looked toward Julian, and beamed. "Then we love the same thing."

"I suppose we do," Julian replied.

Bruno pivoted back to the palette and mixed more paint for the columns. He brushed some paint onto the canvas with an almost dry brush. The paint grabbed the surface of the canvas and the umber under-wash, leaving a column that appeared to have texture.

Julian looked with amazement.

Bruno rolled up his sleeves as the sun rose higher over the small park. The translucent linen shirt dampened as Bruno perspired. He took a long sip of water and offered Julian a drink. "Were you running?"

Julian nodded, took the bottle of water, and took a long sip. He, too, was perspiring and thought it might be time to continue his return home. As he handed the bottle back to Bruno, he detected Bruno's eyes inspecting him, looking first at his torso and then at his legs.

"I should get going. Thanks for letting me watch. I love your work."

Bruno seemed alarmed that Julian was about to leave and said with a sense of urgency, "Would you like to visit my studio. You might find it interesting."

Julian paused and said, "Actually, that would be nice. I would love to see your work."

Bruno took out one of his cards and scribbled an address on the back. "Why don't you come around 6?"

"Thanks. I will."

Julian extended his hand toward Bruno's, and they exchanged a warm handshake. Bruno turned back to the canvas, and Julian pivoted and ran up the slight incline to the street along the Tiber River. He trotted at a light pace under the thick sycamore trees, turned right at the Via Arenula, ran toward the Largo Argentina, and then back to the Piazza Venezia and his apartment.

Once inside, he stripped, took a refreshing shower, and settled in for some work at his computer. Bruno's card laid on the table. After checking emails, he typed in the address for the studio and found that it was located between the Campo de' Fiori and the Largo Argentina, not far from his home.

He dove into the translation of the Ostia codex. He chuckled as he thought about Luciana and her partner, Sofia. "What a surprise," he murmured to himself as he opened the electronic copy of the document and began to decipher the Latin.

Aurelius, the author, began his codex with a brief introduction. He ran a company that repaired ships used for importing goods to

Rome. He had inherited the company from his father. He was married to Adora. Her family had an import business in Rome. Aurelius and Adora had five children and ten servants. Aurelius and his wife enjoyed a good life, and he was happy that Adora was active in the diaconia that the Christians ran near the Foro Boarium.

Aurelius had been classically educated and, although Adora and her family had become Christians, he and his family remained partisans of the traditional Roman religion. Aurelius had a pair of household gods he honored and faithfully offered sacrifices at local temples. Adora insisted their children be raised Christian, much to Aurelius's chagrin.

Julian wasn't familiar with the term *diaconia* and looked it up. Apparently, it was a charity center in early Christianity, a place where food, clothing, and other resources were distributed to the poor. Several were active in 4th century Rome. Later, they became prominent churches.

Aurelius's Latin was easy to follow. He wrote clearly, and his thoughts flowed nicely. Julian looked forward to translating the text and writing a commentary. A few sections of the codex had decomposed, so he would have to see if he could fill in the blanks.

After a couple hours of work, Julian made himself a salad, poured a small glass of wine, and sat in one of the chaises. Aside from the sound of traffic outside the windows, the space was quiet and felt empty. He loved solitude, but the cavernous expanse was overwhelming. The perfectly placed furniture, and carpets, and artwork made it resemble a gallery in a museum, something to look at but not live in.

Marcella filled a room, as did her father, Piero. In years past, when Marcella's parents were alive, Julian's and Marcella's time in Rome was filled with parties, dinners, and social gatherings. After Marcella's death, her friends had reached out to Julian to express condolences, but there had been only tentative suggestions about getting together. As much as Julian had been embraced and welcomed into Marcella's family's circle, now that they were gone, Julian felt sidelined.

Although he loved Rome and felt at home, he wondered if he would ever be an insider again. His daughters loved the city, but they had their own lives back in the States and few links to Italy. His professional connections with Rome were important, and he could envision spending time in the city doing research. But as he looked around the room, it didn't feel like a place he could make his own. It was imprinted with generations of Roman tradition and poised to resist being transformed into something more casual and comfortable.

After more work and a nap, Julian prepared for his visit to Bruno's studio. He slipped into a pair of fresh jeans, pulled a light blue polo shirt over his head, and laced up a stylish pair of suede leather Italian walking shoes. He glanced in the mirror, straightened a few errant locks of hair with his fingers, and gave himself an encouraging smile. He headed out the door and crossed the Piazza Venezia toward Bruno's studio.

The address was more difficult to find than he had expected. He entered a tight maze of short streets. House numbers didn't follow a pattern, at least not one that made sense to him. Eventually, he noticed Bruno's number on a small nondescript doorway tucked in the corner of an old building. He walked up to the dark brown door and noticed a nameplate – Studio Bruno Muzzi – and pressed the buzzer.

A few moments later, he heard someone on the other side of the door unlatch a lock, and the door opened. Bruno stepped forward and shook Julian's hand. "*Benvenuto.*"

"Thanks for the invitation," Julian replied.

Bruno waved him in.

The front door opened into a spacious parlor with a sofa, two upholstered chairs, a coffee table, an antique chest, and several floor lamps. There were recessed lights in the plaster ceiling beaming onto the floor, covered in Persian rugs. The space was classy and cozy.

"This is your studio?" Julian asked skeptically.

"No. My studio is upstairs. This is where I live."

"Ah," Julian said, looking curiously around the room.

"I know. Most people expect to walk into a dingy artist's atelier when they come. I inherited this from my family and converted the top floor to a working space. Come, let me show you."

They climbed a set of stairs just to the right of the front door.

"This is the private area with a couple of bedrooms, baths, and study. Follow me," he said as they continued to another set of stairs.

Julian noticed increased light streaming down the stairwell and, as they approached the top of the stairs, he exclaimed, "Wow! What a space!"

Bruno beamed with delight.

The expansive room had a wood beam ceiling that rose at a steep angle toward a dormer full of windows. "I was able to create an ideal space with lots of indirect light and room."

"I can see that," Julian remarked as he walked toward the center of the area and gazed upward.

Bruno took the back of Julian's arm and said, "Let me show you these."

They walked toward the side of the space where Bruno had a series of easels set up, with paintings resting on each. "These are the ones I have been working on the last week. Recognize this one?" he asked as he pointed to a painting of Trajan's Forum.

Julian nodded. "Indeed. This is the one you did outside my window." He walked up closely and examined it, looking at the brush marks, the detail of the architectural pieces, and the beautiful rendition of the umbrella pines.

Bruno stood behind him. He gazed at the back of Julian's head and followed his closely cropped dark hair as it tapered to his neck. His eyes followed the contours of Julian's shoulders. He breathed in his scent, a subtle citrusy cologne. As Julian turned toward him, Bruno peered into his hazel eyes and felt his legs go weak.

"And this is the one you were doing in the Forum, right?" Julian inquired further.

Bruno nodded, distracted by Julian's lips as he spoke.

"Are you still working on them?" Julian asked, walking toward the one of the Forum.

"I like to work plein-air, but there is always some work to do in the studio. Under studio lights, I examine each piece and make minor corrections. Occasionally, I do a study on site and then come here to do a larger canvas based on the initial sketch."

"Fascinating. I know little about the process of painting. It seems like magic to me. I'm always amazed at how an artist can take something out of the air and bring it to life on canvas."

Bruno smiled. He gazed at the paintings and said, "I guess I'm always surprised myself. It's as if the paintings have a life of their own and materialize before me. I'm channeling the moment and try not to get in the way."

Julian breathed deep breaths through his nose. "I love the smell of paint and oil."

"Most people don't," Bruno noted.

"It feels oddly comforting to me. It's elemental."

Bruno found Julian's observation intriguing. Elemental wasn't a word his friends or acquaintances used. It felt oddly erotic, as if Julian were expressing something primal or sensual. Bruno showed him some other canvases that were dry and framed. "These are for the show in September. I need another ten."

"It looks like you are well on your way."

"I'm always anxious that I won't finish them in time."

"You work quickly. I've watched."

"The initial sketch is quick. I want to capture the essence of the setting as the light is playing on the features of the monuments. But there is more afterwards that must happen – tightening the composition, blending hues, and making sure there are no errors. Then the painting must dry, be varnished, and framed."

"And you do all of that here?"

Bruno nodded. He cleared his throat nervously and asked, "Do you want something to drink?"

Julian looked curiously at Bruno and said, "I don't want to take you away from your work."

"I'm finished for the day. It would be nice to relax and have a drink."

"Well, okay."

"Let's go downstairs," Bruno suggested,

They walked down the stairway and into the parlor. "*Un po' di vino rosso?*" Bruno asked.

Julian nodded, "*Sì, grazie.*" He walked up to the wall to look closely at several paintings. There were a few that were Bruno's, but there were others with a different palette, theme, and style. "Whose are these?"

"They are another Roman artist. Unfortunately, he passed a few years ago. He had such promise."

"Did he die young?"

Bruno nodded emotionally. He went into the kitchen, opened a bottle of wine, poured them each a glass, and walked back into the parlor. "Why don't you have a seat here?"

Julian took one of the upholstered chairs and settled in.

"Are you here on a project?" Bruno inquired.

"Yes. I've been invited to translate and comment on a codex found at Ostia."

"Wow. That's impressive. You must have friends in high places."

"I don't know about that," Julian said evasively. "I just fell into it."

"At the Sapienza?"

"No, at the Capitoline Museums. That is why I was at the Forum the other day."

"Ah," Bruno said nodding.

There was an awkward silence between the two men when Julian glanced at Bruno's wedding band and asked, "Do you live here alone?"

"Yes," Bruno answered without elaboration.

"And you? Where do you live?"

"I live in Atlanta. My family is there."

"Will they be joining you?"

"No," Julian answered.

"That's too bad. Rome is beautiful this time of year."

"Yes. I know. But they have work."

"Children?" Bruno asked.

"I have two college-age daughters."

"And a wife?"

"Yes," Julian replied, not ready to disclose his new status as a widower.

They continued to visit. At one point, Bruno glanced off in the distance as if in thought. He turned toward Julian and said, "Do you have any plans for dinner?"

Julian nodded no.

"Would you like to get something? There's a nice trattoria nearby."

"That would be nice."

Bruno took a long sip of his wine, finishing his glass. Julian followed suit, setting the empty glass on a small side table. Bruno stood, turned off some lights and said, "*Andiamo?*"

"*Sì.* Show me the way."

They walked outside, rounded a corner, and took a narrow lane toward the Campo de' Fiori. Just outside the square, Bruno pointed to a trattoria with a large outdoor seating area. Lights were strung from the roof to poles set along the street. Bruno approached one of the servers who recognized him and asked for a table. The server pointed to one on the edge, and the two men took their seats.

"Is this one of your favorites?"

"Yes. It's a neighborhood place. I come here often."

"That's what I like about Rome. It's a large city made up of small, intimate communities. Everyone knows everyone."

"Sometimes that is a problem!"

Julian laughed.

The waiter approached their table and Bruno ordered wine. He returned and asked what they wanted to eat. Bruno ordered a *saltimbocca con piselli* and Julian ordered a *braciola di maiale* (a pork chop) with *risotto*.

"Your Italian is good," Bruno remarked after the server left the table.

"I've had a lot of practice coming to Rome over the years."

"You obviously have spent some time here."

"A bit," Julian answered, continuing to be evasive. Then he said, "So, what is your favorite setting to paint?"

Bruno looked off into the distance and said, "That's a good question. I guess I would have to say that I like the Roman Forum and the Palatine Hill. There are so many possibilities depending on the time of day and the angle of light."

"I've never seen an artist in front of Trajan's Forum until you were there the other day."

"Yes. It's rarely painted. People like Trajan's column, but the adjacent excavations seem unremarkable. I like to take something that others overlook and bring it to light."

"You do a good job. Did you have formal training?"

Bruno nodded. "I took lessons from several master painters here in Rome. I was going to study architecture. At least that is what my father wanted me to do. I preferred to draw and, after a while, made more money selling drawings and paintings than doing architectural work."

"You don't hear that often. Most artists struggle to make a living, right?"

"Yes, unless you go commercial, churning out tourist pieces."

"And you? How did you end up in classics? That's not a popular field for college students."

"No. It wasn't. My father was a lawyer. I studied history as a prelude to law school. I found I liked history, particularly ancient history. To my father's chagrin, I took more courses in Latin and Greek and ancient history. I loved them. I applied for graduate school and was instantly accepted. Before long, I was on the Ph.D. track and looking for academic positions."

"How did your parents react?"

"At first, not so favorably. But eventually, they saw I was getting lucrative appointments and special grants to study ancient texts."

"So, after the summer, do you go back to the States?"

"That's the plan," Julian said, not convincingly.

Their dinners arrived, and they began to eat. In the soft lights strung overhead, Bruno's eyes were darker and more alluring. As he lifted a fork full of saltimbocca to his mouth, he gazed over his hand into Julian's eyes. Unsettled, Julian evasively looked down at his plate and sliced a piece of pork and push it into a small portion of risotto, lifting the mixture to his mouth.

"Do you have family here?" Julian asked Bruno.

Bruno lifted his wine glass and took a long sip. "No. My parents have passed. I was an only child."

"Are you married – or did you marry?"

Bruno set his fork and knife down on the plate and rubbed his hands nervously. "Regretfully, no. There was someone, but it didn't work out."

"But there must be a line at your door!" Julian said with a bit of jest.

Bruno grinned. "No one compares."

"To whom?"

"Her."

Julian pressed another fork full of risotto onto his fork and lifted it to his mouth. An awkward silence ensued, and Bruno asked, "And your wife?"

"*Una bellezza*," Julian said. "She was so beautiful. She lit up a room. I was so lucky."

"Was?"

"We're no longer together," Julian said, trying to conceal the truth. He felt the information about Marcella's death was too much to share with a stranger, and he was tiring of the pity others showered on him when he mentioned her passing. He thought a different tactic might change the energy, if not for conversations with others, perhaps within himself. It was as if every time he mentioned her death, he felt dead, too. He longed for a new start, for renewed vitality.

"I'm sorry to hear," Bruno said warmly.

"It's okay. Life changes, and we reinvent ourselves."

"If we have the imagination," Bruno added.

"That must come naturally to you?" Julian suggested.

"Yes, I suppose so," Bruno said without conviction.

They continued to chat, finished the bottle of wine, ordered espressos, and strolled back toward Bruno's apartment and studio.

"Thanks for being so generous in showing me your studio. I'm honored."

"It was a pleasure. I sense you have a discriminating eye for art, and I appreciate that. It's also good practice for me to get over the fear I have of letting someone up close to witness the creative process, to see my work in its immediacy."

"You have nothing to fear. It's amazing. It's magical."

Bruno reached over and gave Julian a hug. "*Grazie.*"

"*Grazie a te. Ci vediamo?*"

"Yes, I'm sure we'll run into each other at another excavation. In the meantime, you have my contact information," Bruno added.

Julian turned and walked away. He glanced back, waved at Bruno, and turned a corner.

6

Chapter Six – Ostia Antica

Luciana approached Julian on the platform. She placed her hands on his shoulders, and they exchanged casual cheek kisses. "It's so nice that you were free to meet today. The archaeologists are excited to show you where they found the codex."

"I'm ecstatic. I can't wait," Julian said.

"I see you came prepared for the heat," Luciana said as she noted Julian's baseball cap, long sleeves, shorts, and shoulder bag with bottled water and sunscreen.

"And you as well," he said playfully, waving his hand over her outfit – shorts, sneakers, a light linen blouse, and broad-brimmed hat. "I don't think I've ever seen you outside your professional dress at the museum."

"What about the other night?" Luciana reminded him.

"Ah, yes. The party. We'll come back to that later," Julian said as the graffiti covered train whistled and pulled up to the platform.

The doors opened, and they stepped in, finding two seats facing each other.

"So, how have you been?" Luciana began thoughtfully as the train sped up out of the station.

"I've been busy. There is so much to do with Marcella's estate. It's more complicated than I imagined."

"How are you holding up - I mean with her passing?"

"I'm fine. I thought I would be melancholy, but I'm not. I miss her, and the apartment is so large and empty, with no one around. But, for some reason, I'm okay."

"I've had several friends lose loved ones. When it is sudden, the mourning process is more difficult and intense. If it is a long illness, I believe people are mourning as they watch the other gradually decline and change. You've probably already done a lot of grieving," Luciana explained.

Julian nodded.

"Have you started work on the codex?"

"Yes. It's fascinating. Aurelius is so thoughtful and clear in what he has to say. I think it is going to be a fascinating insight into 4th century Rome. I get the sense that he can articulate and describe how Rome is changing under Christianity and how that is both good and problematic."

"I knew you would be the perfect one to take on this project."

Julian gazed back at Luciana with inquisitive eyes, as if to ask, 'in what sense?'

"You pick up on subtleties quickly. Many can translate Latin technically. You are able to highlight the tone underneath. That is a rare talent."

Julian blushed and shifted the subject. "So, what exactly is going on at Ostia today?"

"There's a gathering of archaeologists to learn more about the discovery of the codex and how this shows the need to continue to excavate areas that haven't been touched or to go back to other areas and finish excavating. It's a way to garner more government funding."

"You know, Ostia was where Marcella and I met."

Luciana reached over and put her hand on Julian's knee. "Oh, Julian. I'm sorry. If I had known, I wouldn't have invited you. I'm sure this will be painful."

"It's okay. I need to go out there and face my anxiety. I've been avoiding it, and perhaps this is precisely the nudge I need."

"If at any point you need to leave, don't hesitate to give me a signal. We can take off whenever you want."

"Thanks. I appreciate it. I will be fine."

"So, how was it you two met?"

"I was on a summer internship with an archaeology class. We were in Ostia, learning about the history of the site and its excavations. Marcella was there with her father at a promotional event for Roman tourism. Piero knew the professor leading our seminar and invited us to join the reception. I literally bumped into Marcella at the buffet. I apologized for causing her to drop some of her food, and she dismissed it, laughing at the incident. She was so affable and full of life. She was gracious, but casual at the same time. She was beautiful – as you know."

"What happened next?"

"Typical of her, she began asking a lot of questions. What was I doing? Where was I from? What interested me in Roman archaeology? We settled into a pleasant exchange as we nibbled on food and drank white wine."

"And?" Luciana pressed. "The good part?"

"Well, we exchanged cards. She invited me to another reception later in the week in Rome. She took the initiative."

"You were the one pursued?"

Julian blushed again. "I'm afraid so."

Luciana looked out of the window as if an insight had overcome her. She looked back at Julian and asked, "Is that when you began to date?"

"We saw each other a few times that summer, but nothing serious. She looked me up on a trip to the States during the school year and, when I was back in Rome the next summer, things heated up."

"And you married shortly thereafter?"

"Well, the engagement was more protracted. Her father wasn't crazy about the idea of her marrying an American, particularly an academic who had a limited fortune."

"I could see that being an issue for him."

"But he also knew Marcella was determined. She was the driving force behind the relationship."

"You must have been interested, too!"

"I was. The idea of marrying into a Roman clan with a long history of promoting Roman heritage was intoxicating – at least for a classicist."

"Yes. I can see that," she said, deep in thought.

"And you?" Julian said, trying to shift the subject again.

"And me what?" Luciana said evasively. "By the way, this is our stop coming up."

The train slowed to a crawl and pulled into a small station set in a grove of pine trees. The doors opened, and they stepped out of the car onto the cement platform. They were the sole passengers getting off at the archaeological site. They left the station and began walking toward the park.

"You were about to tell me about you – about you and Sofia."

"Ah, yes. What do you want to know?"

"Well. I always thought you were into men. You had quite the reputation for partying!"

"I did, didn't I?" she chuckled.

"Hmm, hum."

"Well. In retrospect, I think that was a coping mechanism. I partied, but I kept people at arm's length. If it is all surface, you don't have to let someone in."

Julian nodded for her to continue. They continued to walk along the stones of the ancient Roman road that led into Ostia. Once inside the main gate, the ruins were more substantial, with multi-storied apartment buildings lining the road. Most were nothing more than walls and foundations of bricks, but one could easily imagine the bustling thoroughfare in ancient times.

Luciana continued, "With Sofia, I wanted to let someone in. I didn't feel on guard or defensive. It felt safe and good to share parts of myself that I had kept concealed."

"So, there was a deep connection."

"Yes. And physically, too. That surprised me, but it felt natural. It must be like you and Marcella – you seemed to have had such a good rapport – physically and emotionally."

Julian nodded quietly, looking off to the left at a large structure. He shifted subjects. "So, where are we headed?"

"To the other side of the park, beyond the theater and the Piazzale delle Corporazioni."

"It was in that area that Marcella and I met."

"Are you okay?" Luciana inquired, placing her hand on Julian's forearm.

Julian nodded. They passed between the theater and a large area where ancient Roman businesses were represented by logos embedded in mosaic pavement. Julian loved the pastoral look of Ostia Antica. Unlike Pompeii, which was devoid of trees, the excavated buildings of Ostia were set in grassy fields and shaded by mature umbrella pines. The setting felt alive, and one could more easily imagine life as it had been in late Roman times.

Luciana spotted the group of archaeologists off in the near distance and waved. They walked toward the group, and a tall man gave

Luciana a warm embrace and kissed her on her cheeks. "Luciana, I'm glad you could join us."

"My pleasure. Let me introduce you to Julian. Giancarlo, this is Julian. Julian, Giancarlo."

"*Piacere*," they both said as they shook hands.

"Giancarlo is the superintendent of the archaeological project. Julian is the lead translator and commentator of the codex," she said, first looking at Julian and then turning toward Giancarlo.

"Let me show you where they found the codex," Giancarlo began, waving them to follow him. "By the way, this is Laura and Angela," Giancarlo said as two women joined them. "They were the ones who discovered the manuscript."

"Wow!" Julian said. "That must have been fascinating."

Angela said, "*Sì, veramente. È stata una cosa sorprendente* – really amazing or surprising, I think you say in English!"

They walked toward a cluster of buildings, some with marble still attached to the façade. They walked through a portal and into the interior of the structure. Off to the side was a temporary metal and plastic pavilion covering a dig. They walked up to the edge, and Giancarlo peered over the railing.

"We were digging in this area after finding a few domestic pieces – pottery, metal tools, and jewelry. We then found what looked like it might have been a chest. The exterior was decomposed, but it had a protective interior layer of metal preserving the codex."

Julian peered down into the space, his eyes wide and his mouth open in amazement. "Incredible," he murmured to himself. He took hold of Luciana's hand, emotions coursing through him. The setting reminded him of the time he met Marcella. And he realized he was about to translate a document that had been hidden for over 1600 years.

Luciana looked at Julian and creased her forehead.

Julian asked Giancarlo about the structure and what it might reveal about the codex. Laura had some comments to make about the other items and how they might shed light on the author of the codex as well. After a while at the site, a few workers arrived who were going to continue excavating the area. Luciana, Giancarlo, Laura, Angela, and Julian retreated to the café and had coffee, learning more from Julian about what he had initially discovered in reviewing the codex.

Luciana thanked Giancarlo for his time, and she and Julian headed back to the station to catch a train back to the city. Once on board, Luciana began, "So, what did you think?"

"What an amazing story about the discovery of the book."

"Yes. It's an archaeologist's dream."

"It's also mine – the opportunity to be the first to read an ancient manuscript that has been hidden for centuries."

"I can imagine. I'm happy for you."

"It has come at a good time."

Luciana nodded, as if she had perhaps given him the job in anticipation of the difficult time Julian faced.

Julian then continued, "It is interesting how life throws us curves we never expected. I never imagined Marcella getting sick, much less dying. Now I'm in Rome alone."

"I can't imagine. Is there anything I can do?"

Julian nodded no. "You've been very generous, and I appreciate you welcoming me into your circle."

"Would you like to have dinner when we get back to the city?"

"That would be nice," Julian said. "There's a place behind the Pantheon I like. Let's take the train farther into the city and then walk into the *centro*."

About 40 minutes later, they walked up to a restaurant set near the convergence of several small streets and an intimate piazza. The maitre d' recognized Julian. "*Professor Phillips. Benvenuto.*"

"*Ciao, Allesandro. C'e uno tavolo per due?*"

"For you, the best."

Allesandro pointed to a nice table under an outdoor awning. Patio lights hung from the supports of the canvas. Julian and Luciana took seats, ordered wine, and continued their visit under the soft glow of the lights overhead.

"I'm curious, Julian," she began, "about how your relationship with Marcella began. And forgive me if this is too painful."

"No. It's probably good for me to talk about it - if it's not too boring for you."

"Boring. No way. You were the iconic couple – the daughter of one of the most prominent Roman figureheads and the American classicist. Everyone talked about you."

Julian blushed. "It probably looked more interesting from the outside."

"It always does, but we can still imagine the storybook romance!"

"As I said earlier, Marcella drove the beginning of the relationship. She made the effort to connect here in Rome and in the States. I was shy, into my books, and happy to stay home. She pulled me out of my shell – as you can imagine."

Luciana nodded with a warm smile. "Had you dated before?"

"I went out with a few women here and there. Mostly classmates in college and graduate school. We were all nerds, spending time over dinner talking about research."

"Riveting!" Luciana said jokingly.

"Yes. It must have been. I'm not sure what Marcella saw in me."

Luciana looked off into the distance and rubbed her chin in thought. "Maybe you were the anchor she needed, the stability from which she could do the things she loved."

"Perhaps," Julian replied, nodding as if Luciana's remark made sense.

"Were you in love?" Luciana asked tentatively.

Julian looked at her as if the question were odd. "Of course. Who wouldn't have been in love with Marcella?"

"But was she," and Luciana emphasized she, "in love with you?"

Julian stared at Luciana as if she had gone mad.

"Were the two of you in love?" she repeated unapologetically.

"Why do you ask?"

"Tell me to shut up if I'm getting too personal. It's just that I sometimes wonder if a person in a relationship with someone like Marcella is swept up in the excitement of her life and left unnurtured."

"She adored me and always supported my work."

Luciana smiled, as if she had picked up the scent of something. "You say she loved and supported your work, but what about you, your emotions, your imagination, your dreams?"

Perplexed, Julian replied, "I guess I never really thought about it. My work and academic career were my dreams and imagination."

"I don't buy it. You're more than your work. What satisfies you emotionally and physically?"

Julian stared at her without an answer.

Luciana continued, "When you're not working, and when you are not with Marcella, what do you enjoy? What feeds your soul?"

Julian looked off in the distance, searching for an answer. He began tentatively, "I like to run. I enjoy being in nature. I guess I like art, travel, delicious food. Marcella liked those things, too. We shared an interest in them."

Luciana worried she was pressing Julian too hard, but she wanted to explore one last point. "Describe a situation where you and Marcella were doing something you liked together."

Julian looked down at the table, picked up a fork, and rotated it nervously. "Just before she died, we were at an exhibition at the High Museum of Art in Atlanta. We had special VIP tickets for a prelude event. It was a show of Impressionism."

"Tell me how things unfolded."

"It was during a period of her remission. She was feeling good. We arrived, ordered cocktails, and visited with some friends."

"Hers?"

Julian nodded.

"And?"

"Well, we began to explore the exhibit. There were incredible pieces that had been assembled from collections around the world."

"How did you feel?"

"What do you mean?"

"How did the paintings make you feel?"

"I'm not sure I recall. I was happy Marcella felt good. We kept bumping into her friends as we walked through the gallery, stopping, chatting, catching up."

Luciana had the information she needed. She hypothesized in her mind that Marcella loved being the center of attention, perhaps a need driven by growing up in the shadows of a popular politician. She never let anyone get close enough to detect the sadness and emptiness she felt underneath. And for Julian, Marcella must have provided the simulacra of a relationship, doing all sorts of exciting things together, but never sharing emotional intimacy since, as Luciana suspected, Julian was probably afraid of his own emotions and Marcella's were concealed and painful. Luciana could only recognize this in the light of her own self-discovery and wondered how long it would take after Marcella's passing before Julian faced a crisis of his own.

"That must have been exciting," Luciana said. "Do you miss that?"

Julian nodded.

"I think I asked you this before, but do you think you'll begin dating again?"

Julian fussed nervously with the fork in front of him. "I'm not sure. I suppose so, but I'm in no hurry."

"I told you the other day, I can make some introductions," she said with a bit of playfulness, raising her eyebrows.

"Yeah, like Luca and Stefano?"

"Well, I can introduce you to women, too."

"What kind?"

"The kind that would be interested in you!"

Julian smiled bashfully.

"That settles it, we'll have to have a casual party soon – one that doesn't put any pressure on you or anyone else. If some chemistry arises, it won't be forced!"

Julian creased his forehead as if in disbelief.

"What? You don't think I can organize a party that doesn't have an agenda?"

"Not really," Julian said matter-of-factly.

"Then you know me too well."

Their meals arrived. They continued to visit as they ate. Afterwards, they ordered espresso, brandy, and leaned back in their chairs to enjoy the sensual night air of Rome.

Eventually Luciana broke the spell and said, "Well, I think I might need to head home. It's late, and I have a long day tomorrow."

"Me, too. I'm hoping to make headway on the codex."

"You know, you don't have to finish it this summer. Take your time. Enjoy Rome. You have a lot to get over, and Rome is the perfect place to sooth the soul."

Julian nodded.

They both stood, embraced, gave each other kisses.

"Thanks so much for today," Julian said. "It was wonderful to spend time with you."

"Me, too. I enjoyed it. And, when you're ready, I can make introductions."

Julian gave a thumbs up, smiled, and turned to head toward his apartment as Luciana began walking the other way.

7

Chapter Seven – A Commission

Julian woke in the middle of the night, startled by an intense dream. It wasn't particularly disturbing. Rather, it was remarkable for its vividness. Marcella was standing amongst a group of friends, laughing, gesturing, and placing her hands affectionately on her friends' shoulders, arms, and hands. At one point, she glanced over her shoulder, caught Julian's eye, and winked.

Julian smiled and nodded, and then turned back to a small group of people assembled around him. He faced Luciana. As he spoke to her, her face morphed into Bruno's. Julian blinked, hoping Luciana would return to focus, but Bruno remained. He wanted to say something to him but was at a loss for words and awoke.

"Wow!" he said to himself as he slowly roused from a heavy torpor. A streetlamp cast an orange glow on one side of the room. As things came into focus, Julian recreated the scene in his mind. "It was so realistic," he said to himself. It was the first dream he had of

Marcella since her death. It was as if she were physically present in the room. He wished he had said something to her.

He got out of bed and went to the kitchen to pour a glass of water. It was 3 AM, and he wondered if he should turn on lights and do some work or go back to sleep. He chose to work. As he opened the codex, the setting of the dream became clear to him in a flash, a reception held at Ostia Antica. He quickly recalled a large tent set on the lawn near the theater and people milling about, sipping cocktails. Marcella's presence made sense as it was where they first met, and it did not surprise him to see Luciana as they had just visited the archaeological site a few days before. But Bruno's appearance was surprising. He glanced over and noticed Bruno's card laying on the side of the table. He picked it up and turned it over between his fingers.

Later that morning, he called Bruno and reached his voicemail. "Bruno. This is Julian. Can you call me at your convenience? I would like to see if you might do a commission for me."

Bruno returned the call later that afternoon, inviting Julian for a drink. At a small wine bar near his studio, they met, shook hands warmly, and sat down at a small table, awkwardly beginning a conversation.

"How have you been?" Julian began.

"Good, thanks. And you?"

Julian vacillated between feeling a familiarity with Bruno and maintaining a certain formality. On the one hand, there had been the intimacy of dinner, sharing a drink in his home, and watching him paint on site. But he barely knew him, one of Rome's most illustrious painters. "Where have you been painting this week?" he asked.

"On the Palatine. The light was brilliant this week."

Julian widened his eyes as if impressed, nodded, and said, "Wonderful. I'm sure it must be satisfying when things come together."

"Yes. It doesn't always happen, but when it does, it's rewarding. And you?" Bruno asked. "How's your work?"

"It's going well. I went to Ostia Antica to see the place where they found the codex. It was quite emotional."

Bruno gazed at Julian warmly, picking up on his excitement. He let one of his hands rest on the table, near Julian's, feeling heat radiating from it.

Julian continued, clearing his throat, "That's why I called you. I was wondering if you might consider a commission for a painting of the site?"

"Of Ostia?"

Julian nodded.

"Do you have something in mind – a particular structure or setting? There is so much there."

"I was thinking of a scene near the base of the theater, near the Piazzale delle Corporazioni."

"That's a nice setting. Is that where they found the codex?"

"No. It's just sentimental for me."

Bruno raised one of his brows and said, "That is a nice area. I like the trees, the columns, and various architectural elements that can be woven together in a painting."

"I figured you could come up with a unique composition. You have such a good eye. You see things that are overlooked – or at least you can bring into focus things that most of us miss."

Bruno wrung his hands nervously, and Julian creased his forehead in alarm as Bruno spoke. "I generally don't like to do commissions. I don't like to paint in anticipation of what I think someone else wants."

"I understand. Sorry," Julian apologized. "I thought I would at least ask."

"Don't apologize. I wouldn't have invited you for a drink if I wasn't going to give it consideration." He grinned at Julian.

Julian sighed in relief and moved to the edge of his chair in anticipation of what Bruno was about to say. Bruno said nothing. He reached for his glass of wine and took a sip. He looked deep in thought. Impatient, Julian interjected, "What if you were to do a painting of Ostia for your show, and if I liked it, I could buy it in advance? No pressure then to paint for me."

Bruno set his glass back down on the table and looked off into the distance. He then spoke slowly and thoughtfully, "I wanted to include a piece or two from there in the show. This might be the impetus to do something. Why not?"

Julian smiled contently.

Bruno gazed at Julian and sensed there might be more to his interest than the codex. "While I don't want to paint for you, it might be nice to visit the site with you and see if there is some synergy, some common impressions that might inform the piece."

"I wouldn't want to be a bother to you or impede the creative process."

"You won't be a bother. I haven't been to the site in a few years, and I would savor the opportunity to explore it with an archaeologist's eyes."

"I'm not an archaeologist. I'm a classicist."

"What's the difference? Both are trying to make sense of the past," Bruno said, raising his eyebrows playfully.

"Point made," Julian said as he chuckled.

"What are you doing day after tomorrow? We could go to the park in the morning when light is more interesting."

"That works for me. I'm flexible."

"Would you be up for a picnic on the beach afterwards? The weather has been great, and I have missed the opportunity to lie in the sand and enjoy a swim."

Bruno's suggestion caught Julian off-guard. It felt more familiar than a transactional visit to an archaeological site. He was hesitant, fearful he might disappoint Bruno, not confident of his own conversational abilities in a protracted casual outing.

"Hmm. It has been a while since I've been to the beach at Ostia. Why not?" Julian agreed reluctantly.

"Perfect. Is 7 AM too early for you? At the Ostiense station?"

"No. That's great."

"*Allora*, it's a date." Bruno said enthusiastically.

Nervously, Julian responded, "*Sì, ci vediamo dopo domani.*"

They finished their wine, stood, embraced, and walked their separate ways.

Two days later, Julian stood outside the station, waiting for Bruno. It was hazy, foreshadowing a warm sunny day later. Large crowds of people exited the station, coming into the city for work. A cab pulled up to the sidewalk, and Bruno stepped out. He waved warmly at Julian.

"*Ciao. Come va?*" Bruno said as he approached.

"*Bene, e tu?*" Julian replied.

"I'm good. Will it be sunny later?" Bruno asked, looking nervously at the sky.

"This will burn off. It will be a nice warm sunny day."

"*Andiamo?*" Bruno asked as they both walked into the busy station.

Bruno walked just slightly behind Julian, observing him carefully. He recalled having seen his lean runner legs a week ago and couldn't help but note his legs had become tanner and the dark hair running down his upper legs and over his calves more pronounced. His blue running shoes complemented his dark blue shorts and a peculiar but striking peach-pink hued polo shirt.

"I see you've come prepared," he began, nodding toward Julian's baseball cap.

"Yes, even with the shade at the archaeology site, I imagine it will be sunny at the beach. Did you bring a suit?"

Bruno lifted his shoulder bag slightly. "It's in here – with a towel and lunch."

"Me, too," Julian added, glancing at his own canvas shoulder bag.

They walked to the platform where a train pulled up quickly, disgorging suburban passengers. Julian and Bruno joined a handful of passengers making the reverse commute. They stepped into a car and took seats opposite each other.

"Thanks for doing this," Julian began awkwardly.

"I'm not doing it for you, remember?" Bruno said with a grin.

"Yes. You're right. We're just scoping out a setting for a piece in your show."

"*Appunto!*"

Bruno had a warm smile. On site, while painting, he had always seemed remote, as if in another world. Julian imagined the artistic process required concentration and focus. Now Bruno gazed at him and seemed eager to engage. He was a man of few words, but his eyes were intense and filled with curiosity. They were dark brown, deeply set, and encircled by dark brows and thick lashes.

Julian felt self-conscious and looked nervously out the window.

"I thought you were from Atlanta. Isn't that a Red Sox cap?" Bruno remarked.

Surprised by Bruno's attention to detail, Julian said, "Yes. I was born in the northeast."

"Are you a baseball fan?"

"Not really. I was never into sports. I guess I preferred books. And you? Soccer?"

"Only when our team is winning," Bruno said, chuckling. "But you're a runner, right? Even with the books, you seem to have time to work out," Bruno noted, trying to find topics with which to connect with his new friend.

Julian had never considered it odd that he was a scholar and athletic, but now that Bruno asked, he said, "Yeah. I suppose you're right. It is odd."

"It's not that peculiar, though. Running is a solitary sport."

Julian nodded, amazed at how observant and penetrating Bruno was. Bruno reached into his bag and pulled out a small bottle of water and took a long sip. He reached over to offer Julian a sip. He declined. A few drops of water dropped onto Bruno's leg, just between his knee and the edge of his shorts. Julian watched as the drops clung to a few wisps of dark hair and slowly disappeared into the dark folds of his shorts.

Bruno had a handsome face framed by a trimmed beard lining his strong, jutting chin and circling his mouth. The upper buttons of his linen shirt were unfastened, revealing the edges of what Julian imagined being a muscular, hairy chest.

"And you, do you do any sports?"

"I work out at the gym. And I have the advantage of being on my feet a lot when I paint."

Julian nodded. "I guess my occupational hazard is just the opposite – sitting too much. Perhaps that's why I run."

"What does your ex do?"

"You mean in terms of sports?"

"No – her occupation."

"Ahh," Julian began. "Philanthropy."

"That's interesting and unique. Where? In Atlanta?"

Julian nodded nervously and then shifted the subject quickly, asking, "And your family? Are you from here? Are your parents still alive?"

"Yes. I'm from Rome. I have two sisters. My parents are deceased."

"I'm sorry. Do you see your sisters much?"

"They've moved away and have families. We see each other at holidays."

"You mentioned two daughters. Will they come visit you this summer?" Bruno asked.

"I'm hoping so. They like Rome a lot, but they also have their lives and a boring summer with dad isn't what they had in mind."

"But you can take them to the beach. What's better than a week or two in August at an Italian resort?"

"You're right," Julian nodded. "We used to do that when they were younger." The mention of summers past was jarring, a painful reminder of Marcella's absence.

Bruno creased his forehead as he watched Julian slip off in thought.

Shortly, the train pulled into the Ostia Antica station. They both gathered their bags and exited the car. They walked toward the main gate of the archaeological park.

"How are we going to get in?" Julian asked, realizing they had arrived earlier than the official opening of the site.

"I know the superintendent. He's arranged for the guard to let us in."

Julian sighed. "Whew. I didn't even think."

They approached the official entrance of the park, and Bruno spoke to the guard who waved them in. They walked through the ancient Roman gate and into the excavated city. The air was hazy and dense and filtered the morning light into ethereal rays that glistened on the dewy grass.

"I always love the smell of Ostia Antica," Bruno began as he breathed in heavily. "The salt air mixed with fresh grass and an earthy scent rising from the old buildings."

Julian was struck not so much by the aroma of the surroundings but by the deafening silence of their solitude, two souls walking through a dead city. With no distractions, he felt as if generations of residents were clamoring to be heard, to be noticed, to be felt. He imagined voices greeting one another as they went about their business - neighbors, merchants, soldiers, slaves, and children - elbowing each other through the busy thoroughfare. He must have slipped into a trance since suddenly, he felt Bruno's hand grab the back of his arm. "Are you okay? You looked like you were getting dizzy."

Julian regained composure and said, "Yeah. I'm fine. I guess I was just picking up on the vibes of the place. It's so still without people here. It's easy to imagine another time."

This didn't surprise Bruno, who had a vivid imagination. It was one reason he loved to paint Roman sites. Julian's confession only reinforced Bruno's interest in eliciting Julian's impressions as the basis of a new painting.

They walked toward the theater and the Piazzale delle Corporazioni. There were many structures in the area, the temple of Ceres (the Greek goddess Demeter), the theater, and foundations and columns behind the stage. Mature umbrella pines shaded the large Piazzale. Other substantial structures one would have expected nearby, surrounded the theater.

Bruno was already piecing together elements for a nice painting, observing how the light created shadows and reflected off columns, architectural pieces, and the surrounding landscape. Julian looked over and noticed Bruno's head pivoting back and forth.

"Are you getting some ideas?" he asked Bruno.

Bruno nodded. "And you? What do you see?"

Oddly, he felt the urge to say, 'A very creative Roman painter,' but he resisted and said, "From what you've painted before, I can imagine a scene with this row of columns catching the morning light. The pine trees in the background would offer a nice backdrop."

Bruno smiled. "Yes. I see that. But do you see that piece over there?" He pointed to a capital that had fallen and was lying on the ground.

Julian squinted his eyes and nodded.

"It could be the focus of the painting with the columns and trees more of an impressionistic background. Sometimes there are little things we overlook that can form the anchor of a whole sensation or impression."

Bruno reached into his bag and pulled out a sketch pad. He took a soft pencil and sketched quickly the architectural element. He shaded it as the light would and roughly added trees and columns in the background.

"Wow!" Julian exclaimed as he gazed at the sketch, his mouth agape. "All that from that small piece of marble and stone?"

Bruno nodded proudly. He then sketched a setting with the columns, a more traditional composition of the site. "What do you think of this?"

The setting was familiar to him. It framed the setting for his meeting Marcella twenty-five years ago. He wanted to blurt out, 'That's it. That's perfect. It's amazing.' But he glanced back at the sketch of the unremarkable architectural element and was intrigued. There was something haunting about it – a lone piece of marble aching for attention from the margins.

Bruno could tell Julian was conflicted. He said, "Let's walk around and do some more sketches. We don't have to settle on anything now. By the way, can you show me where they found the codex?"

"This way," Julian said, waving Bruno forward. They meandered through a few roadways and in and out of some excavated buildings including a Roman apartment building, a bathhouse, and what best could be described as a brasserie where people gathered to visit, drink, and nibble on food.

"Over there. See the pavilion?" Julian said, pointing to the protective covering of the site.

They walked toward the space and peered over. Bruno asked, "So, they found it here?"

"Hmm, hum. It was in a wooden chest that, fortunately, had an interior lining that protected the parchment."

"Amazing that things like that come to light after so much time. Do you expect it to reveal anything new?"

"Apparently, the author, Aurelius, was married to Adora. Adora was a deaconess in early Christianity. From what I can gather, Aurelius was impressed with the charitable outreach of the Christian community, but he was alarmed at how monotheism eroded away at religious plurality, something he considered a foundation for Roman civilization."

"That's fascinating. I would imagine for an American, that would be an interesting study given the political landscape in your country."

"Indeed. I wonder if it won't be interesting for Europeans, too, who seem to struggle with similar questions around immigration."

Bruno nodded. "So, you've always been interested in ancient civilizations?"

"Yes. Although my curiosity strengthened during college."

"And your ex. Was she supportive?"

Julian nodded. He found it increasingly difficult to conceal who his wife was, or that she had passed, but he stayed the course and maintain the story he had woven. "She was. She liked all things Roman."

"That must have been convenient for you."

The word 'convenient' startled Julian. It shattered a myth he had constructed about their mutual interests and synergy, realizing that perhaps Marcella had been intoxicating precisely because she was the daughter of a prominent Roman and a lucky break for a classicist. Although she had pursued him, he now wondered if his response to her had been more opportunistic than romantic.

Julian nodded. They left the pavilion and continued to walk through the excavations. The haze burned off, and a pleasant breeze blew from the nearby shore. A few tourists emerged as the park opened. Julian observed Bruno, who focused intently on the landscape, scrutinizing every angle for elements or a grouping that would form the basis for a compelling composition.

"How do you decide what to paint?" Julian asked gently, not wanting to intrude on Bruno's inner process too abruptly.

"I like settings that showcase the contrast between light and shadow, as you probably already know from my work. The composition needs to have some kind of movement, something that draws the eyes toward whatever is the focus. A lot of artists search for triangular shapes where things narrow toward a particular object. I like elements that have texture. Most importantly, I search for something that evokes nostalgia – places that stir something dormant, places that invite us to see ourselves differently."

"How do you do that in a painting, without commentary?" Julian asked.

"Remember the painting I did at Trajan's Forum?"

Julian nodded.

"Most people go there to see Trajan's column. The excavated area with columns is seemingly unremarkable. I wanted to focus the attention on the place where people used to gather and conduct business in ancient times. The sunlight illuminated the space and, with the umbrella pines in the background, the scene is animated; it comes to life. People can see themselves there and ask who they might have been or what they were doing."

"Wow! That's amazing," Julian remarked. "Classicists have an easier time. We let the authors – the texts - tell the stories and invite people in."

"But most people don't read the classics. They don't see the relevance. Isn't that part of the challenge of your work, to inspire contemporary people to explore ancient books?"

"It's an acquired taste. I don't have any illusions about making the classics popular."

"Then why study them?"

"So that we know history; so that we can document what happened," Julian said matter-of-factly as they strolled along a stone road between two ancient apartment buildings.

Bruno had a different perspective and said, "If I ask you what happened in your life, if I ask you to document your past, is a catalogue of facts sufficient for me to know you? Where you grew up, what schools you went to, what you did, who you knew, what languages you spoke, and what religion you professed don't tell me how you made sense of those things on the inside. And as we continue to mature, the only way we grow and evolve is if we can reinterpret our past in new ways."

Julian nodded, as if what Bruno was saying made sense, but it didn't.

"I am not the product or outcome of a series of happenstances and data. Sure, they are influential, but ultimately I am who I am in the way I connect the past with the future as I stand in the present."

"You lost me," Julian said.

"You're reading a 1600-year-old manuscript. It's likely to include a lot of interesting details about ancient Roman life. I'm sure other classicists will salivate to get hold of your work."

Julian grinned.

"But what I find fascinating about the codex is not a snapshot of the past but an event that we enter."

"But now you're talking about fiction, imagining some interior process that may or may not be true. We have to stick with the facts."

"But that's not what any human being is. Humans are not facts. Humans are not nouns. Humans are verbs, events, imagination. I want my paintings to inspire imagination and personal creativity."

"I get that. Art is imaginative and creative. History is about documenting the past, about facts."

"Life is fiction. It is the process of authoring our lives," Bruno said with conviction. "It's not just art or novels that are fiction, everything is an act of imagination and creativity."

Julian still didn't comprehend what Bruno was saying, and the glassy look in his eyes begged for Bruno to continue.

"The translation of the codex isn't an academic chronicle of the past. It was the author's imagination that gave it shape and form, that looked at events in his day with fresh eyes. But the event – his creative process – isn't past. It continues. You are now taking part in that event. You will see what he said with new eyes, too. And just as Aurelius imagined his future and Rome's future, this event will invite you to author your future and our future."

Julian's heart skipped a beat as Bruno said, 'our future.' He wasn't sure if Bruno meant it in the collective social sense or in a more intimate interpersonal sense, and the ambiguity startled him. Had he missed some clues? Did Bruno have ulterior motives in their getting together? He scrutinized Bruno's face for clarity. Bruno remained inscrutable, his eyes darting back and forth at the landscape, occasionally pausing as he observed Julian.

They circled back to the theater. There had been several scenes that spoke to Bruno, but he sensed Julian was still drawn to the Piazzale delle Corporazioni. "Has anything grabbed you?"

"I keep coming back to this setting."

"I noticed it moved you earlier. It's nice. I can do a nice painting."

"But what inspires you?" Julian pressed Bruno.

"I like the columns and the trees, but that broken capital on the ground keeps beckoning to me. There's something wanting to be noticed and highlighted."

"What do you think that is?"

Bruno stood quietly, contemplating the architectural fragment.

He squinted his eyes and then closed them. He opened them again. "It used to crown a structure. It tied things together, connecting columns and roof. Now it is solitary and devoid of utility. It is beautiful in and of itself."

As Bruno concluded, Julian felt an intense connection with the piece, as if he became the piece. He was sad. He had exerted so much effort holding things together, supporting his family, connecting people – his wife, her family, their kids – and now, like the marble piece, he was solitary. Bruno's concluding words – 'it is beautiful in and of itself' – were haunting. He knew he should embrace them as a foretelling for his life, as a way to celebrate attractiveness without defined function, but he couldn't do it. He turned toward the line of columns and the well-identified contours of the theater and the surrounding structures and said, "I like the architectural piece, and I get what you are saying, but it's not enough."

Chapter Eight – The Free Beach

Bruno pressed a button to signal their stop, and the bus slowed as it approached a rusted sign along the road. He and Julian walked to the front of the bus, nodded to the driver, and stepped onto the hot asphalt pavement. The bus pulled away, and they walked toward an indentation in the dunes, following a path of footprints in the yellow sand.

"And where are we, exactly?" Julian asked Bruno as he followed him past clumps of dune grass waving in the gentle breeze.

"The *spiaggia libera*. It's the free beach. I'm not a fan of the commercial set up at Ostia Lido. I like the pristine sand, water, and sky that one can enjoy here just a kilometer or two south."

Julian glanced around. He and Marcella had rarely gone to Ostia Lido, preferring their friends' villas at San Felice Circeo or a more extended vacation along the Amalfi Coast. If they went to the beach near Rome, they would have taken a car service to one of the upscale establishments where they could rent cabanas, chaise lounges, and order cocktails.

The free beach had a primitive beauty to it – irregular dunes, soft yellow sand that stretched as far as the eye could see, and sparkling blue water lapping at the shore. There were more people than Julian had imagined, clusters of bathers huddled under the shade of umbrellas or lying in the sun on towels. A few were swimming.

Bruno scanned the beach and said, "What about over there?" He pointed to an open section of sand off to the right.

Julian nodded, and they both marched forward, weaving their way through bodies lying in the sun. Julian observed that most were men and wondered if it wasn't a gay beach. They found their place. Bruno extracted a towel from his bag and laid it carefully on the sand. "I'm sorry I didn't think to bring an umbrella. It's likely to be sunny later."

"That's okay," Julian replied. "We can always take a refreshing dip in the water – or head back to town when we've had enough."

Bruno sat on his towel as Julian remained standing, looking up and down the beach. "It's so beautiful," he remarked. "It's not unlike the beaches near Atlanta."

"Do you go often?"

"We used to go more often, but I don't seem to find the time. It's a long drive from the city."

"This is so convenient to Rome, but I don't come often," Bruno remarked.

Bruno unbuttoned his shirt, took it off, and rolled it carefully into his bag. He laid back on the towel, resting his head on his hands, crossed behind him. Although Bruno had mentioned he worked out, Julian was surprised by how sculpted his torso was. He had a taut abdomen and well-defined pecs covered in thick but trimmed dark hair. Julian sat down on his towel and lifted his long-sleeve tee shirt over his head. He replaced his cap, put on dark glasses, and pulled his knees up to his chest, and looked out over the horizon.

"Is there a place to change into our suits?" Julian asked.

"Not here," Bruno replied. "People are uninhibited. They just change on the beach. It's pretty casual."

Bruno unzipped his shorts. He reached into his bag and retrieved a thin black Speedo suit. While still seated, he pulled down his shorts and undershorts and placed his feet into the legs of the suit. As he extended his legs, his large, dark, uncut penis came into view. Julian tried not to stare, but found it difficult not to make an initial assessment of Bruno's attributes.

Bruno pulled the suit up to his waist and adjusted himself and laid back down on the towel. He glanced over to Julian, who seemed anxious.

"*Ma dai*, don't be bashful," he said playfully, encouraging Julian to put his suit on.

Julian reached down and grabbed his towel, wrapping it around his waist. He unzipped his shorts and let them drop to the ground. He pulled his own suit out of his bag and, from under the towel, stepped into it and pulled it up snuggly to his waist. He placed the towel back down and laid on it.

"You Americans are so modest," Bruno said as he reached over and nudged Julian's shoulder.

"We are, aren't we?"

Bruno nodded. "Like look at your suit. How is that any different from a pair of walking shorts?" he asked, referring to Julian's boxer-style trunks.

"Different material."

"Oh, I see."

Bruno gazed at Julian's legs, lean, dark, hairy. He found Julian's swimsuit oddly erotic, the billowing legs teasing him to reach up and explore his runner's thighs. He felt himself get hard and rolled over to conceal his erection.

Julian glanced over. He found it difficult to avoid noticing Bruno's broad muscular back and his firm, round buttocks. He propped himself on his elbows to take in the view of Bruno's physique and the sparkling water beyond.

"There seem to be a lot of guys here," Julian remarked. "Is this a gay beach?" he asked pointedly.

Bruno was taken aback by Julian's directness and chuckled. He said evasively, "We Italians avoid categories, but I'm sure there are some gay people here."

"Why is that?"

"Why is it that there are gay people here or that we avoid categories?"

"Both."

"Well, the *spiaggia libera* is precisely that – a free beach – where people can dress or undress and be who they want to be without the confines of a more formal beach establishment."

"And categories?"

"Italians are more comfortable with ambiguity than Americans."

"What does that mean?" Julian pressed Bruno further.

"One's sexuality isn't always so well-defined. It's not an either-or kind of thing. There's fluidity to physical desire."

"Is there? Or is it that some people are afraid to embrace their sexuality?"

"It could be both," Bruno answered, raising his brows.

Julian leaned back and reached into his canvas bag for some water. He unscrewed the top of the bottle and took a long sip. He offered some to Bruno, who nodded no.

Julian had grown up in the northeast during a time when people felt constrained to declare their orientation one way or the other. There was little ambiguity and, when someone professed to be bisexual, it was usually only a matter of time before they dated people of their own sex exclusively.

He always preferred women, although as a runner he recalled checking out his teammates' physiques in the locker room. But he assured himself, everyone did that. Given his own build and size, he was envied and feared. No one ever approached him. Once he and Marcella began to date, he never questioned his orientation. Sex with her was contagious. She had full round breasts, dark silky skin, and loved to caress and suck his erection until he was throbbing, and then have her pleasure with him. In retrospect, he realized he rarely took the initiative.

Luciana's newly declared interest in women unnerved him. He was intrigued by how the desire to weave a protective shield could drive sexual behavior. He always thought he and Marcella had a good relationship, but now he wondered if they had both found ways to protect raw and tender feelings.

"Are you hungry?" Bruno asked.

Startled out of his thoughts, Julian nodded. He stretched toward his bag and pulled out a sandwich and some fruit. Bruno sat up and reached into his bag, doing the same.

"What did you make?" Julian asked.

"Chicken with pesto. And you?"

"Prosciutto and mozzarella. *Ne vuoi un po*?"

Bruno nodded, and Julian tore a piece of his sandwich and gave it to Bruno, who offered Julian a piece of his. They were both sitting facing each other, their legs crossed.

"This was a great idea," Julian interjected. "It's nice to get out of the city and enjoy the beach. It's such a change of pace."

"I can spend a day here and feel like I've been on vacation for a week."

Julian nodded as he took another sip of water.

"You mentioned someone the other day, a girlfriend. What happened?"

Bruno shifted nervously. "It just didn't work out."

Julian didn't follow up, waiting for Bruno to elaborate. He didn't.

"How long ago?"

"A long time – perhaps thirty years."

"Hm," Julian murmured. "And after her?" he asked, looking directly at Bruno's ring.

Bruno noticed, glanced at it, and said, "I wear it to dissuade people. It makes life simpler."

"And others?"

"No one, really. No one has ever compared to her. I'm waiting for the right one."

"What was she like?" Julian pressed.

"Full of life. Affable. Beautiful. Charming. Sophisticated."

"Sounds phenomenal."

"Yes. But unattainable."

"But surely you are a catch."

"Hm," Bruno murmured. "I'm not so sure."

Julian wondered what the problem was. Bruno was handsome, successful, charming, and engaging. What woman wouldn't have snatched him up?

They finished their sandwiches and laid back down on the sand. The sun was bright and warm, and Julian savored the way it caressed his skin. There was just enough breeze to keep them comfortable, and he found himself ready to doze off.

"Do you mind?" Bruno asked quietly as he tugged at his suit, ready to take it off.

Julian nodded no.

Bruno slipped his Speedo off and turned over on his stomach, his buttocks glistening in the sun.

"You know, you can take yours off, too," he said playfully.

Not wanting to be prudish, Julian slid his trunks off, rolling them up as a pillow on the edge of his towel. He laid on his stomach as well.

"That's better. Tan lines are overrated."

They both chuckled.

Julian fell asleep to the gentle sound of the waves washing on the shore. Later, he was awakened when a couple with a dog passed nearby. He turned his head toward Bruno, who was now laying on his back. Small beads of perspiration were forming on his temple just above his thick brows. His head was tilted back, his chin jutting into the air. He watched Bruno's chest rise and fall with each breath.

From Julian's perspective on the ground, he could only see Bruno's side. He was curious, turned himself over and propped himself up on his elbows to observe Bruno's penis. It was firm and full, but not erect or aroused. He felt the sun warm his own penis and felt a slight stirring. He had never been to a nude beach but had to admit the freedom to hangout in the sunlight and on the sand was liberating.

A couple of men nearby kissed. One of them wore a Speedo, but his erection was clearly apparent. The other was turned toward his partner, his buttocks flexing as he nuzzled himself close. Julian found the scene surprisingly arousing, his own shaft hardening as he watched them play with each other.

Bruno stirred, opened his eyes, and looked over at Julian, whose erection glistened in the sun. Julian felt Bruno's gaze and sat up, pulling his legs up close to his chest, concealing his hardness. Bruno followed Julian's stare to the couple nearby and, as he watched, he became aroused as well.

"*Vuoi andare in acqua?*"

Julian nodded, stood, and started to put on his suit for a swim.

"*Ma dai, senza costume.*"

Julian, embarrassed, dropped his suit as Bruno commanded and walked toward the water's edge. Their erections dissipated as they approached the water. They waded in, the briny water silky and soothing. They swam out to deeper water and treaded in place, letting the waves wash over them.

"This feels so good," Julian remarked.

"I love the freedom of swimming without a suit."

"I have to admit, it's nice."

"The water is unusually warm for this time of the year," Bruno remarked.

A few guys ran toward the water and leaped in, swimming past them and pushing each other down playfully in the water. They kept eyeing Bruno and Julian as they continued to frolic in the water. Julian noticed Bruno looking and asked, "You mentioned the Italian comfort with ambiguity earlier. Any men?"

Bruno pivoted toward Julian, realizing he had been staring toward the nearby group, and said, "No. It doesn't bother me, but no. What about you?"

"The same."

Julian sighed, relieved that he and Bruno were seemingly on the same page. He took several strokes away from the shore into the cooler and deeper water. He dove to the bottom, ran his hand along the coarse sand, picked up a shell, and returned to the surface, showing it to Bruno.

Bruno swam toward him and treaded in place. Julian's hazel eyes were piercing, framed handsomely by broad brows and a tall forehead. He had a warm smile and a slightly protruding lower lip that became more pronounced when he spoke – particularly in Italian.

"How did you learn Italian so well?"

Evasively, Julian said, "In graduate school."

"*Non è possibile.* You can't learn the Italian you speak in school."

"I came to Rome several summers for seminars and archaeological work."

"Ahh," Bruno noted, "that makes more sense. So, you've spent time here."

"A fair amount," Julian said, concealing how much.

They continued to chat and tread water, then Bruno said, "I'm getting tired. Should we head back to shore?"

Julian nodded and swam toward the shore. Suddenly, he felt Bruno grab his ankles and tug at him. He felt Bruno swim over and past him, challenging him to a race.

"*Cazzo!*" Julian said uncharacteristically, reaching for Bruno's legs. He grabbed hold of one. Bruno tried to kick free, but Julian hung on and got hold of the other. He pulled himself up on top of Bruno and dunked him under water, racing off quickly as Bruno tried to recover.

Julian reached shallower water and lowered his feet to the ground. Bruno had followed him and was now pushing briskly through the water toward him. He grabbed hold of Julian's shoulders and tried to pry his feet from the sandy bottom. Julian lost balance and fell back into the water.

Bruno offered his hand to lift him up and Julian took advantage and pulled Bruno down with him. They both stood up and splashed each other playfully. Julian felt self-conscious as his cock bounced up and down in the air. He dove toward deeper water and swam away. Bruno followed suit. They both placed their feet on the bottom, with the water lapping at their chests.

"You're a formidable opponent," Bruno remarked. "All that jogging is paying off."

Julian grinned. "You're not so bad yourself."

"Shall we?" Bruno said.

"*Senza interferenza?*"

"Yes, without interference," Bruno agreed, amazed at Julian's vocabulary.

They wandered toward the shore and their towels and stood in place as they dried themselves. Julian found it difficult to avoid gawking at Bruno as he leaned over to dry his legs, flexing his buttocks and upper legs. He eyed Bruno to see if he was eyeing those around them, searching for clues that might reveal more about his artist friend. He still wasn't convinced that the choice of the *spiaggia libera* was entirely casual or coincidental.

Bruno was on his best behavior, keeping his roving eye in check. He was disappointed that Julian didn't seem to have any hidden closets he was ready to open, but he was certainly not reluctant to shed inhibitions. And he had a hot body – taut, lean, and smooth.

"You ready to head back to the city?" Bruno inquired.

"Sure. I think I've had enough sun."

Bruno reached down for his shorts and pulled them on. He slipped his arms in the linen shirt but left it unbuttoned. He rolled up his towel and stuffed things into the canvas bag. Julian did the same, slipping on his shorts, pulling the polo over his head, and fastening his sneakers. They walked across the beach toward the roadway to wait for the next bus that would take them to the metro station at Ostia Lido.

When they arrived at Ostiense, Bruno said, "Should we get something to eat?"

Julian pondered the question and said, "That would be nice, but I'm dirty from the beach. I should go home first and change."

"You can come to my place. It's nearby. We can clean up and then go out for a pizza or something."

"My place is as close as yours. Why don't we just meet up later?"

Julian could see the disappointment in Bruno's eyes, but really wanted to go to his own apartment. Bruno's resourcefulness surprised him. "I'd like to show you the pieces I did of the Palatine. Why don't you come over? I have a clean shirt you can borrow."

Julian nodded reluctantly and followed Bruno to his place. They walked inside. Bruno turned on lights and led Julian upstairs.

"You can use the bathroom down the hall. There are fresh towels in there. And here," he said as he tossed him a blue polo shirt he pulled from a closet in the hallway, "You can wear this."

Julian caught the shirt in the air and headed down the hall. He turned on the shower and stepped into the warm water. It felt good shedding the salt and sand from his skin. He looked down and realized he had picked up a good deal of sun, his skin turning dark brown. He dried himself, rubbed his fingers through his hair in the absence of a brush, and rinsed his mouth with some water. He slipped the polo shirt over his head. It fit nicely, snuggly. He pulled up his shorts and slipped on his sneakers. As he walked down the hall, he peered into Bruno's bedroom. He was standing in front of a mirror, holding a towel to his forehead, his buttocks and back in full view. Julian lingered for a moment, then continued down the hall, down the stairs, and sat in one of the large chairs in the living room. Soon, Bruno followed.

"It felt good to clean up," Julian said.

"Yes. You ready to go?"

"Weren't you going to show me the paintings of the Palatine?" Julian reminded him.

"Oh, yes. I almost forgot. Let's go up."

Bruno led Julian up to the studio and showed him his latest work. One of them was not unlike the concept Bruno kept suggesting at Ostia Antica – a lone architectural fragment as the center of a composition. Julian said, "I like this. I didn't think I would."

Bruno smiled. "I thought you might. It's haunting, isn't it?"

"Yes. I don't know why."

Bruno continued to stare at the piece, smiling contently. "Yes. It seems to have a unique personality – if one dare says an architectural fragment could be personified."

"Isn't that what you long for in your work – that people can see themselves in the pieces?" Julian inquired.

"Yes, I guess you're right. But this one seems odd in that sense," Bruno noted. He gazed at the piece, then turned toward Julian.

"*Andiamo?*" Julian suggested.

"Yes. Let's go. I'm starving."

9

Chapter Nine – Excavations

Bruno unpacked his paints and brushes and leaned the canvas on the easel. He found a piece of shade under which to stand with the architectural fragment resting in the nearby sun. There was a haze in the air, making it easier for Bruno to imagine a more impressionistic background.

The capital laid at the edge of a clay walkway lined with dry yellow grass. Just beyond the fragment there was a verdant green lawn and stately umbrella pines. Bruno blocked in some of the darker background and idealized the lines of the walkway so that they pointed toward the lone piece of brick and marble.

He mixed several colors together to create the white he would use for the marble, a warm white, one that represented morning sunlight with hints of vermillion and permanent rose. He tentatively sketched the piece with a thin brush and gray paint.

Quickly the composition came together, and Bruno was confident it would proceed as envisioned. While Bruno usually did some initial sketches to guide his work, he had learned to let the paintings lead the way – a process where light, shadow, and form appeared as if by magic. He felt as if he were a channel for something wanting to be revealed.

The architectural fragment at Ostia was, as he had remarked several times, haunting. Even Julian noticed it. He wasn't sure what that meant, but he expected that as he worked, something would come to him.

He stood back, squinted, then refocused. He had managed to get the values of light and shadow down nicely, and he was happy with the texture and movement of elements. He took a break, reaching into his canvas bag for water. He took a long sip as tourists gathered, looking at his work.

He chatted with some visitors from other parts of Europe and many from the States. He watched a squadron of archaeologists march nearby, probably heading to the active site where they found the codex. He thought of Julian and wondered what he discovered as he read Aurelius's journal.

He laughed as he recalled their day together. Julian was so modest and shy and seemingly uncomfortable with sexual ambiguity. As they dined and Julian talked about his family, Bruno wondered if he wasn't certifiably straight. He was the classic scholar – buried deep in his work and oblivious to the efforts of others to seduce him.

He set his water bottle down on a ledge and turned back to the painting. An odd sensation washed over him – one he hadn't experienced in some time. It was an uneasiness with the canvas in front of him. He was convinced that capturing the solitary piece was key to a unique work, one that would not only satisfy Julian, but impress his fans as well. But the more he got into the work, the less certain he was of how to finish it.

He peeked at the palette. His customary colors weren't working.

He would need to mix new hues. The angle of light was off. He could fix that. But he couldn't decide how tight or loose to make the lines. He continued to work on the piece but became increasingly unhappy with it. He looked at his watch and realized it was time to return to Rome. He wrapped his brushes, covered the palette, and slipped the canvas into its holder. He returned home.

Once inside his studio, he looked at the painting again, and decided it wasn't working. He heard that some artists throw out 10 to 20% of their paintings – pieces that just aren't working. Bruno hadn't tossed anything in years. It unnerved him, but he shredded the canvas and started over.

The next day, he returned to Ostia Antica to begin again. He got to a certain point and struggled as he had the day before. He glanced over at the columns nearby and the umbrella pines in the distance and realized he could whip out something quickly – a painting that his patrons would snatch up right away. He pulled out a fresh canvas and began painting the columns. The composition came together as if by magic. He finished his session, wrapped his brushes, and returned to his studio, where he would eventually finish the work.

He had invited Julian for a drink to see the progress of the work. Around 6, Julian rang his buzzer. Bruno appeared at the doorway and smiled warmly when he saw him. They embraced, and Bruno led Julian upstairs.

"I think you are going to be surprised," Bruno began. "I went back to the original idea."

They reached the top of the stairs and walked into the studio space. Julian breathed in deeply the comforting smells of oil and paint. Bruno turned on some lights and grabbed hold of Julian's hand, leading him to the canvas. Julian extracted his hand and stood in front of the painting.

"I thought you were going to do the architectural fragment."

"I was. But it wasn't working. It must not have wanted to be painted. It resisted me."

Julian, always the critical scholar, thought in his mind, 'or you were resisting it.'

"It's beautiful. I love how you've captured the morning light at Ostia – how it catches the morning haze and filters through the grass and trees."

Bruno smiled.

"It's perfect," Julian said again reassuringly. It reminded him of the time he met Marcella. It was a fitting memento – not only capturing the place but highlighting their interest in ancient Rome.

"Do you have time for dinner?" Bruno suggested.

Julian projected a surprised look on his face, as if Bruno's suggestion were unanticipated. It wasn't. "That would be great. I'm hungry."

They turned off the lights and walked outside. The air was temperate, as it often is in Rome in early summer. They strolled to a nearby trattoria and found a table outside.

Bruno ordered wine, and they toasted to his work. "Again, the painting is marvelous," Julian reiterated.

"Yes," Bruno murmured. But he wasn't at peace with it. It upset him that he hadn't been able to do something outside his comfort zone, beyond a set formula he had developed over the years. He felt troubled. Julian noticed.

"You look unsettled."

"I am a little. I guess I am disappointed that the other composition didn't work. I tried it twice. Ordinarily, I would just say – it's not the right composition. But you were there the other day. The sketched worked. It should have been possible. I don't know what's wrong."

"Maybe I impeded your artistic process. Maybe subconsciously, you were painting for what you thought I wanted."

"Perhaps," Bruno said, not convinced that was the issue.

They ordered their dinners and continued to visit. Bruno talked about the upcoming show, and Julian recounted what he had discovered in the codex. Bruno then asked, "Are you going to date?"

The question surprised Julian. He looked off evasively, then turned back to Bruno. "I don't think I'm over my ex yet." He maintained the narrative he had begun with Bruno.

"She must be quite something that you aren't over her yet. Did she break up with you?"

"It was mutual."

"Oh. That's tough. No acrimony."

Julian chuckled. "What about you?"

"My friends have been trying to set me up. They're good intentioned, but they don't seem to understand my type."

"What is your type?" Julian inquired.

"I keep going back to her. She was so beautiful – caramel skin, dark hair, thick lashes. She was full of life and filled a room. He made me want to be my better self. I've never felt that with anyone else."

"What about good enough?" Julian asked. "Are we sometimes trying to chase a phantom, an idealized person who doesn't exist?"

"I'm okay waiting. I'm in no hurry," Bruno said thoughtfully, but Julian's statement troubled him, as if he had accidentally put his finger on something.

Julian glanced over at Bruno and remarked to himself that he wasn't getting any younger and that while he looked good, he was approaching the age where starting a family was increasingly impractical.

"I haven't been single for so long. I'm not sure where I would start," Julian mused.

"What's your type?"

"I'm not sure I have one. I dated little before I met my wife. There's not much of a pattern."

"Maybe I can get some of my friends to fix us up with a couple of women. It would be fun.," Bruno offered, continuing to maintain the straight façade he had projected but hoping Julian would never take him up on it.

"Thanks. But I think I'm okay for the moment," Julian said.

"Well, when you're ready, let me know."

Julian nodded.

They finished their dinners and wine. They strolled down a narrow lane to a small café, had a couple of espressos and a brandy, then parted ways. Julian walked back to his apartment, and Bruno went to the Lungo Tevere, the road that ran along the Tiber River. Occasionally, he would bump into another solitary soul and hook up for an anonymous encounter – a quick *scopata* – with a man.

Bruno liked more masculine types. That evening, the Lungo Tevere was more of a runway for drag, so he slipped into an inconspicuous bar that catered to men and noticed someone across the room. Bruno approached and offered him a drink. Aldo was thirty and looking for money. Bruno wasn't opposed to paying for sex, but it startled him that he had been singled out as older and would have to pay.

Aldo had dark hair, a smooth face, and deep alluring eyes. He smelled good and knew how to put on the charm. He complimented Bruno's sculpted chest and his firm buttocks and before long, Bruno had invited him to his apartment. Aldo was well-endowed, and Bruno felt like he got his money's worth after their exchange.

The next day, Bruno spent time in his studio. He had several pieces he needed to clean up before he could frame them and include them in the show. He sorted through materials and organized some files. The sketch book he had taken to Ostia Antica was lying on a side table. As he picked it up to tuck it in with other books filled with drafts, he glanced at the architectural fragment he had outlined the week before. The sketch seemed to glare at him, almost in mockery.

He wanted to bury it, but resisted, fearing it would be like burying himself. "I have to face this. I have to paint this."

He pulled out a fresh canvas and prepped it with a burnt umber wash. He mixed some paint and began a few tentative strokes. "Ah, that's good," he said, noting the dramatic contrast of the bright pigment with the dark background. "Now," he said to himself, "let go. Feel the piece."

Inside, he visualized a little boy waving a brush back and forth. This made him nervous since the architectural fragment had lots of detail he wanted to capture. He closed his eyes and watched the boy. The boy stood before a dark void, his hand guiding the brush wildly across the space.

Bruno closed his eyes and let his own brush move spontaneously across the prepared canvas, letting go of the fear of not capturing the details of the capital. He felt the brush move over the surface, roughly in accord with the general shape and form of the piece. When he opened his eyes, he was surprised at what he saw. He fully expected chaos. Instead, he had somehow captured the subtleties of the piece, the pigment and brush strokes having skimmed over the dark canvas in surprising ways.

He thought immediately of Julian and dialed his number.

"*Pronto*," Julian answered.

"Julian, this is Bruno. Can you come to my studio right away?"

"Sure, is something the matter?"

"No. I just want to show you something."

Julian put his work aside, freshened up in the bathroom, and walked briskly toward Bruno's apartment. He rang the bell, and Bruno let him in, grabbing his hand enthusiastically, leading him upstairs to the studio.

"Look!" he exclaimed as he approached the new canvas.

"Wow!" Julian said. "When did you do this? How did you do this?"

"I was frustrated. I was doing some other work, and I gave it another try."

"What did you do differently?"

"I let go. I know this sounds crazy with, what do you say in English – a lot of psychobabble – but I let my inner child paint. I just let him go."

"He did a good job. It's amazing. I love how the loose brushstrokes and the bright hues give the architectural piece a lot of texture and even detail."

"I had to get out of my comfort zone and let something inside take over," Bruno said.

"But I thought that's what artists do anyway," Julian interjected.

"Yes, and no. There's a certain letting go. But there's also one's tried-and-true palette and subjects and techniques. It becomes formulaic at some point."

"I suppose there are breakthrough moments, when artists enter a new period," Julian observed.

Bruno nodded thoughtfully, then he said, "I have an idea. I think I need to find an entirely new venue for painting – change things up a bit."

Julian was alarmed. Bruno was successful, and he wasn't sure a new technique or palette or theme would be good for business. "Are you sure? What about your show in September?"

"I have enough for that, already. I want to see if I can take the next leap."

"What do you have in mind?"

"Seascapes."

"Seascapes?" Julian exclaimed, creasing his forehead.

"Yes. I've always envied those who could paint seascapes. I love cascading shorelines, turquoise water, boats, piers, and the hazy horizon. I have a friend who is always offering me her villa in Capri. It's still early in the season, and I'm sure it's available. We could go for a few days to get out of Rome and try something new.

Julian stood dumbfounded in front of Bruno, not sure how to react. The idea of an excursion to Capri sounded appealing. He could use a bit of a break, an escape from the deafening silence of Marcella's parents' apartment.

"Sure," he said tentatively. "Why don't you get in touch with your friend and let me know what works. I'm flexible."

Chapter Ten – Capri

The fast ferry pulled up to the marina in Capri. The port was not remarkable, given the otherwise exotic landscape and luxurious accommodations of the island. It served as a point of entry for tourists, day trippers, and an occasional yacht looking for a few hours of mooring. There was an active fishing community, as evidenced by dozens of small colorful boats tied together and loaded with nets. Julian and Bruno pressed forward through the crowd of tourists from Naples and Sorrento and negotiated a decent fare with a local taxi driver for a ride to Bruno's friend's villa.

Julian had been to Capri years ago with Marcella and her family. Bruno had never been. Bruno's face was glued to the taxi window as they wound their way up the steep roadway toward the center of Capri proper and then down the other side of the island toward the Marina Piccola. Bruno was amazed at the contrast between scrubby vegetation and rocky terrain with magnificent gardens and villas tucked away here and there. As the road wound tightly up and down the mountain, views of the sea below came into view, and Bruno gasped with excitement. Twenty minutes later, they pulled up to a gate on a narrow road. "This is it," Bruno said as he glanced at the address on his phone and then back up at the number on the fence post.

Julian's eyes widened as he surveyed the elegant building perched on a narrow terrace between the roadway and what he imagined was a steep drop off on the other side. Bruno paid the driver, and they wheeled their suitcases to the front entrance. Bruno opened the door, disarmed the alarm, and walked inside. "Wow!" he exclaimed as the grandeur of the space became evident. "Marianna always told me it was spectacular, but I never imagined."

The main floor was spacious. It included a grand parlor surrounded by arches leading to a dining area, kitchen, study, and bathroom. Decorative ceramics covered the white plaster walls. The floors were blue and white tile on which Marianna had positioned comfortable sofas, chairs, coffee tables, and floor lamps.

Everything faced a wall of windows and glass doors leading to a deck overlooking the Mediterranean. Bruno and Julian were silent as they made their way onto the balcony and felt the gentle breeze blowing up the mountainside, carrying with it the aroma of rosemary and native brush. Julian took a deep breath and sighed, "My God."

"Sì, Dio mio," Bruno echoed.

The water stretched out before them, a luminescent expanse of turquoise and blue fading to a hazy horizon. A few sail boats drifted across the gentle sea.

Bruno looked down at the garden below. "There's even a pool. Marianna never mentioned it."

Julian peered over the edge of the balcony and surveyed the garden on the lower level. "Let's go look," he said, dragging Bruno with him.

They walked through the master bedroom and out onto a marble deck and up to the edge of a spacious pool. Chaise lounges were lined up in the sun, and a large lemon tree shaded a cabana with an outdoor shower and bar. Bruno looked at Julian. "Can you believe this?"

"What does your friend do again?"

"She's a cultural minister. I think this has been in her family for generations."

"And how do you know her?" Julian pressed.

"We worked together on some art projects in Rome."

"It's very generous of her to let us use this. It's amazing."

"Why don't we unpack and explore?" Bruno suggested.

Julian nodded. "Which room should I take?"

Julian's question caught Bruno by surprise. He had never really thought about sleeping arrangements, although the idea of sleeping with Julian was clearly on his radar. Their relationship was undefined and budding. It had been ages since he traveled alone with a friend and hadn't really considered what the proper protocol was – whether there might be an expectation to share a room or not. "Ah, yes. Maybe you can take this one. I'll take the one down the hall."

"You should have this one. You're Marianna's friend."

"Whatever you'd like. Let's just get unpacked so we can explore."

Julian went down the hall, opened the door to another suite, and unpacked his bags. He put his toiletries in the bathroom, washed up, arranged his hair, and went back down the hall to Bruno's room. Bruno had just about finished unpacking. He set his easel and painting materials inside a side closet and was adjusting his shorts and shirt.

"Ready?" Bruno asked.

"Sure. Where are we heading?"

"I don't know. You want to just walk – perhaps down to the small port?"

Julian nodded.

They went upstairs and out the main entrance, following the windy road down toward the water. Views of the sea and the rugged coastline below were breathtaking. Several massive rock formations rested just offshore, giving the landscape an even more exotic allure. As they approached the small port and village, there were more apartments, inns, bars, restaurants, and decks on the shore lined with chaise lounges, umbrellas, and tan bodies.

They found a welcoming restaurant overlooking the harbor, grabbed a table, and ordered a bottle of crisp white wine and seafood appetizers.

Bruno looked out over the horizon and smiled contently. He gazed at Julian and said, "Thanks for coming. I'm not sure I would have done this alone."

"Are you kidding? Thanks for including me. This is spectacular. I hope you can find inspiration for your work."

"I can feel it," Bruno said excitedly. The light was different and more intense. He would have to add red and vermillion pigments to add warmth to the elements in his composition. The shadows were less elongated but more intense, and he imagined how he might add violet hues under rocks and brush.

"I'm still curious about what is driving this," Julian began thoughtfully.

"I don't know. It was the experience of hitting a wall, realizing I had gotten stuck in a rut, and wanting to let my inner child loose."

"That's wonderful. Don't let me get in the way."

"You're the reason I'm embarking on this. If you hadn't pushed me, I wouldn't be here.

Julian blushed.

After appetizers, they ordered seafood risotto and a salad. The waterfront was active, with private motorboats coming and going, picking up and letting off passengers on excursions around the island. At a nearby inn, guests were sunning on chaise lounges and swimming in the transparent blue water.

After lunch, Julian said, "How about a dip in our pool? I'm ready to soak up some sun and relax from the train and ferry this morning."

"Me, too," Bruno said.

They paid their bill and climbed the hill back to the villa. Once inside, they put on their suits and stepped out to the pool and arranged the chairs to face the sun. Bruno draped a towel over his chair, leaned the back lower, and laid down. His skin gleamed in the bright sunshine. He glanced over to Julian, who sat down on the edge of his chair, took a sip of water, and then reclined as well.

Bruno chuckled. "You and your American trunks. You're going to have a nasty tan line."

Julian glared at Bruno from behind his sunglasses.

"Pull them off," Bruno said emphatically. "I need inspiration."

"I thought you were doing seascapes," Julian replied.

"Well, you might be surprised. I'm going to follow inspiration where it takes me this weekend."

Julian felt alarmed by Bruno's blatant forwardness.

Bruno could see Julian's panic and said, "Sorry. Don't mind me. I'm just glad to be away from Rome for a break. I get silly sometimes."

Bruno's levity was out of character, a shift from his customary ponderous, pensive, and absorbed demeanor.

Julian didn't respond. He was tired from travel, and the wine from lunch was kicking in. He closed his eyes and fell quickly asleep. Bruno was restless, eager to ride the creative energy coursing through his body. He tried to close his eyes to rest, but his mind was racing. He glanced over at Julian – calm and serene. He seized on Julian's slumber to scrutinize his body undetected. Julian had classic English features - a tall forehead, dark wavy hair, angular jaws, and a sinewy frame. As a runner, he had little body fat. His chest and abdomen were lean and smooth. His skin tanned easily as evidenced by his dark legs covered in wispy black hair.

He had already seen Julian's cock – one that was certainly generous in dimensions and expanded considerably when erect. He was still uncertain of Julian's proclivities. He had been married until recently and was clearly shy, perhaps even prudish. But oddly, he had agreed to travel with him and was now lying only inches away at the side of a pool overlooking the exotic landscape of Capri.

Julian stirred. He lifted himself up, took a sip of water, and looked out over the garden, the pool, and the ocean beyond. The setting was magnificent, with rocky hillsides plunging into crystal clear water. Their secluded terrace was perched on a natural outcrop, affording unobstructed views and privacy. He stood, dropped his trunks onto the deck, and jumped into the water.

"*Cazzo!*" Bruno murmured to himself, taken aback by Julian's bold move. He slipped his Speedo off and jumped in behind him.

"It feels good, no?" Julian said.

"*Veramente,*" Bruno replied, turning over on his back and gazing at the blue sky above. Julian treaded toward the other side and stretched his arms along the marble edge of the pool. Bruno joined him, both gazing off into the distance and letting their nude torsos float gently just below the surface. Julian felt himself get aroused at the sight of Bruno's body and turned to face the side of the pool.

The sensation was troubling and new, but not off-putting. He found Bruno appealing and mysterious. When his erection had subsided, he pulled himself out of the water, wrapped himself in a towel, and laid back down on the chaise. Bruno swam a couple of laps and climbed out of the pool, strolling around the garden to dry. He returned to the chaise and laid on the towel. A few remaining drops of water ran down his chest and onto the dark hair surrounding his cock. His chest swelled as he breathed, and his skin gleamed in the bright sun.

Julian reached casually for his phone and checked for emails and messages. The sun was warm, so he removed the towel and let the light caress his skin. He felt Bruno's eyes turn toward him. He turned toward Bruno and smiled.

After a few moments, Bruno stood up and sat down on Julian's chaise, his firm buttocks pressed against Julian's side. The gesture was intimate and provocative, but since he was facing away from Julian, it was loaded with ambiguity. Bruno intended it so – physical intimacy laced with the pretext of casual camaraderie.

Bruno pivoted slightly, crossed one of his legs over his knee, and nonchalantly offered Julian some water. Julian nodded no. Bruno took a long sip, some of the water dripping onto his chest. Julian starred at the glistening drops resting on the coarse, dark hair of Bruno's chest. After a pause, he leaned over and ran his fingers tenderly and deliberately over the water to wipe the drops. It was a simple but profoundly intimate gesture, and Bruno seized it. He leaned over and gave Julian a tender kiss.

Julian pulled back at first out of surprise, then leaned forward, placed his hand behind Bruno's head, and pulled him close. They both breathed each other in, exploring the moist space between them. Bruno's lips were full and warm. He moved his mouth down over Julian's chin, then along his jaw, and then licked the inside of Julian's ear with his warm, moist tongue. Julian felt himself become aroused, his cock becoming hard and erect.

Bruno stopped, pulled his and Julian's sunglasses off, and stared into his eyes. "*Che sorpresa!*"

Julian just nodded, not wanting to break the spell with words. He knew his tendency would be to analyze things, to second guess himself, to ask questions, but now all he wanted was for Bruno to take the lead. He would follow.

Bruno was about to say something, and Julian placed his fingers on his lips and whispered, "Shh."

Bruno lifted his right leg over Julian's, pressed Julian's legs apart, and sat between them, facing him. He wrapped his own legs around Julian's waist, feeling the hardness of their cocks pressed against each other. Bruno caressed Julian's chest and tugged playfully at his nipples. Julian pulled Bruno closer and higher onto him, placing his hands under Bruno's firm, round buttocks and squeezed them. Bruno arched his back, pressing his hardness into Julian's taut abdomen. Julian could feel intense heat emanating from Bruno's flesh. He opened his mouth and let Bruno plunge his tongue deep within.

Bruno was riding the ecstasy of the passion between them, but a little voice in the back of his head signaled alarm. 'Not so fast. This is new to him. It could backfire.'

He wanted to push Julian back on the chair and dangle his engorged cock over his face, hoping he would bath his hardness in hot saliva. He was ready to reach down and take hold of Julian, stroke him till he moaned, and bring him to climax. The little voice in his head said, 'Find a way to cool this.' It was an alien message; one he would have disregarded in the past.

"What a hottie," he said playfully to Julian as he inched away. Julian took hold of Bruno's cock and stroked it.

Bruno preemptively took hold of Julian's hand and clasped it tightly. "You're so handsome."

Julian blushed.

"And an enigma," Bruno added.

Julian creased his forehead. "In what sense?"

"Well, this was all pretty much unexpected."

"Come on. You've been trying to draw this out of me for the past week," Julian said, still convinced Bruno's excursion to the beach at Ostia was a test run.

"I was getting pretty discouraged. You're a hard nut to crack."

"You're persistent," Julian said, nudging Bruno playfully.

"So?" Bruno murmured protractedly, letting the word float in the air in search of an explanation.

Julian looked off evasively, still not sure he was ready to cool their exchange. "I'm curious," was all he could say, looking down at Bruno's legs and erection spread in front of him.

"Is that what you call it?" Bruno said playfully, leaning toward him and giving him a chaste kiss.

Julian ran a hand over Bruno's round, muscular shoulder and squeezed his bicep. He could feel his own cock vibrating, craving to be held. He reached down and stroked Bruno, who grabbed his hand and said, "Later."

Julian pursed his lips in a pout. Bruno ran his fingers affectionately over Julian's mouth and said, "I want you to take me for a walk. We need to explore. I want to see this place through your eyes."

Julian creased his forehead.

"You're my muse," Bruno said, half in jest and half seriously. "Come on. We need to shower and get dressed."

Julian now questioned his initial hunch. Maybe Bruno wasn't that into men, and he, Julian, had crossed a line. They stood, draped towels over their shoulders, and went inside to shower. A while later, Bruno walked upstairs to find Julian resting on the sofa, looking out over the horizon.

"Are you okay?"

Julian nodded. "Yeah. Let's go. The sun is lower on the horizon, and there could be some nice light. There are some trails nearby, including one that leads to the ruins of Tiberius's villa, Villa Jovis."

They walked outside and found a trail that led toward the Via Krupp, a classic road running along the south coast of the island. Once on the roadway, they found little paths that led to cliffs overhanging the water.

"Oh my God," Bruno exclaimed as they carefully navigated a

steep rocky trail and approached a ledge hanging over the water. "It's magnificent."

Julian followed him and stood back from the edge, apprehensive of the height.

"Look at the shoreline!" Bruno exclaimed. "It's so - what did you say the other day – elemental!"

Julian nodded. "Yes. There's something about the rocks, the scrub vegetation, and the water – hues of white, blue-gray, green, and turquoise blue. Looks like a painting to me," he said to Bruno.

Bruno shook his head. "I'm not sure. Yes. It's magnificent, and for many, it would make for a marvelous piece of art. But it's just beautiful. It says nothing."

"Does art have to say something? Can't it just be beautiful?"

Bruno rubbed his chin and continued to gaze at the landscape, at the way the rocks plunged into the sea and how vegetation clung to crevasses and was shaped by the wind.

"My work has to say something. It can't just be pretty. It has to tug at the soul."

"Hmm," Julian murmured. He had always been impressed by Bruno's evocative work, but he was having a tough time combining thoughtful art with the hot body he had just touched. "Do you have any ideas about how to create something like that here?"

"Look over there," Bruno said, pointing to a craggy overhang. "See that scrub pine tree?"

Julian nodded.

"Look how the branches have been shaped by the wind. The main trunk of the tree leans toward the wind, toward the water, but the branches are nimble and curved backward. It's a substantial tree that has survived storms, heavy rains, and crumbling earth. Its roots must be deep, searching for soil and moisture. I can imagine a composition with the tree in the foreground, perhaps off to the side, and the craggy shoreline, water, and sky forming a triangular shape."

Bruno held his hands up and formed a frame, squinting at the tree in the near distance. "Yes. That could work."

"And the message?"

"It's a metaphor for our lives. We cling to things that root and nurture us as we face adversity. Life is beautiful and rough. Horizons draw us forward. Life shapes us. Our past is gnarly."

"So, you're a poet as well."

Bruno blushed. "It's all about imagination. Life is art."

Julian gazed at Bruno as he continued to frame the setting with his hands. It was fascinating to get into the mind of the artist. He never realized how much went into a painting.

Bruno was proud of the thoughts that leaped off his tongue. He wasn't sure where they came from, but he was pleasantly surprised. His body ached for Julian, and perhaps he was taping into that current of desire. It had taken every ounce of self-control to slow things down. He knew Julian felt it, too, but it was a whole new experience for Julian and, if he didn't manage this carefully, he would scare him off.

11

Chapter Eleven – Advice

"*Pronto*," the silky voice on the other end of the line answered.

"Marianna, it's Bruno. *Come stai?*"

"*Bene.* Is everything alright? Any problems at the villa?"

"Everything is magnificent. What a place. I never imagined."

"It is nice, isn't it? I'm glad it worked out. Any new inspiration?"

"Yes, but that's not what I'm calling about. I need your honest tough-love advice."

"Okay. Now you've got my attention. What's up, *caro*?"

"I'm in love."

"No!" Marianna exclaimed in shock. "*Non è possibile.*"

"*Sì.*"

"With the professor – what's his name?"

"Julian. *Sì.*"

"How did this happen? I had entirely given up on you."

"I don't know. There's something there," Bruno said slowly.

"Is he gay?"

"That's the problem. I don't know."

"What happened to your gaydar? Have you had sex?"

"Almost."

"What happened?"

"I put the brakes on."

"You did?"

"Yes. I know it's hard to believe."

"Well, if he was about to do it, then he's part of the tribe," Marianna said playfully.

"That's what I thought, but I've caught him cruising women, and he doesn't seem to be over his ex."

"He's divorced."

"Hmm hum."

"Why do you think you're in love? Are you sure you just don't have the hots for him?"

"I crave his body. He's cute and sophisticated at the same time. He's age appropriate. He's playful, affectionate, thoughtful, and able to have interesting conversations. And, most importantly, he gets my work."

"And you haven't done it yet?"

"I don't want to spoil it. You know me – a quick *scopata* – and I'm off to the next."

"I've been meaning to talk to you about that. It's dangerous," Marianna said pointedly.

"I know. I can't seem to settle down."

"I'm going to say something. Don't get upset."

"Go ahead," Bruno said with reluctance.

"You keep holding onto your relationship with what's her name, as if it proves you aren't gay. You put her on a pedestal that no one could ever match, trying to assure yourself that if only the right woman came along, you would marry and have kids. Honey, that train left the station a long time ago. You need to admit to yourself that you love men. Your father is gone. You can let that demon go. Embrace the beautiful person you are and let someone love you."

Bruno said nothing.

"Bruno?"

"Yes – I know you're right. I'm not sure I'm ready," he said pensively.

"When will you? Yes, you're handsome. But you're not getting any younger. You might want to think about a change in strategy."

"I'm scared."

"Why?"

"I'm crazy in love with him. If I let go and dive in, and he doesn't reciprocate or gets scared and runs back to women, I don't think I could deal with that rejection again."

"Love is always risky. We become vulnerable – that's the whole point."

"But I don't think I could deal with the hurt again. It was too much. It has been too much," Bruno reiterated.

Marianna didn't respond. There was a protracted silence, and Bruno nervously continued, "So, what do you think?"

"Hmm," she murmured. "I'm not the most appropriate one to give advice. Look at me."

"But I know you'll tell me the truth, even if it is painful."

"Well, I've never heard you talk like this before. So, something is different in a good sense."

"Go on," he said anxiously.

"How long was he married?"

"Apparently twenty-something years. He has two daughters in college," Bruno noted.

"It's not out of the question for someone to come out late in life. It sounds like you both have some work to do in that area – although you have a head start," she said, laughing.

"Be kind!"

"I was!" she said with emphasis.

"Give it a go. What do you have to lose?"

"Him."

"Honey, if he races back to women, then you never had him in the first place. If you end up being friends and not lovers, what's the problem with that?"

"Frustration!" Bruno said with a slight chuckle.

"I'm sure you can find a little hottie to take care of that," she said, laughing again.

"It's not funny."

"Sorry. Why don't you give it a try? Take it slow. Get him to talk."

"He's coming," Bruno whispered to Marianna as Julian approached him in the garden.

"*Ciao, caro.* Let me know how it goes."

"*Ciao.*"

Julian walked up to Bruno and said, "Who was that?"

"Marianna. She called to find out if everything was in order. She had the caretaker stock the refrigerator and wanted to make sure we had seen what was in there."

"I hope you thanked her. It was nice to wake up to a cup of espresso and granola."

"How did you sleep?" Bruno asked.

"Great. The bed is so comfortable and it's so quiet. I read a little and fell quickly asleep. And you?"

"The same," Bruno said.

Both Julian and Bruno avoided extended eye contact and weren't sure where to take the conversation. They had enjoyed a nice dinner the night before but avoided mention of the incident at the pool. Julian was perplexed. Bruno seemed so turned on and then, all-of-a-sudden, cooled things. He wondered if Bruno might not be as fluid as he let on or that maybe he wasn't that attractive.

"Are you going to paint today?"

Bruno nodded.

"Do you need some help setting things up?"

"I thought I might try the area we identified yesterday afternoon. I think I can handle it. Will you be okay on your own today?"

Julian nodded. "Sure. I thought I might hike or run."

"Perfect. Then we can get together later for drinks and dinner?"

"Sure. I think I'm going to change and go out before it gets too warm."

"Me, too," Bruno said.

They went back to their respective rooms. Bruno prepared his paints, and Julian quickly changed into his swimming trunks and headed out the door. He had heard of a bathing establishment and restaurant overlooking the Faraglioni – large rock formations just offshore. He calculated it would be a pleasant run, so he ran toward the Via Krupp and followed the coastline toward the far end of the island. It was an arduous route of winding roads and steep inclines. He reached the restaurant and terrace and paid the attendant for a chaise, umbrella, and towel.

The setting was striking. A rocky terrace overlooking the Faraglioni and coves of clear blue water had been converted into a deck for bathers. Julian pulled off his tee-shirt and shoes, reclined the back of the chair, and laid down in the sun. Chairs filled, and well-heeled clientele began to order espressos, fruit, and cocktails.

Julian began to perspire and decided to take a dip. He walked to the edge of the terrace and leaped off into the crystal-clear water, swimming out toward the rocky formations. The briny water felt soothing and refreshing. He treaded back to the terrace, climbed the ladder, and lowered the back of the chaise further and laid down on his stomach.

He closed his eyes and listened to the cacophony of languages – the playful sound of Italian, the guttural tones of German, the soft accent of the French and, of course, the ubiquitous English –

predominantly American. A nearby couple ordered espressos. The woman's voice was loud and obnoxious with a heavy southern drawl. A server approached Julian, who, in perfect Italian, ordered a salad and a glass of wine.

A man on the adjacent chair looked up over his newspaper, surprised that Julian, clearly an American, had ordered in Italian. He smiled at Julian, who smiled back.

Earlier, the man had placed a book on Julian's table. "*Scusi,*" he apologized as he reached for it. He took the book and placed it under a saucer on his own table.

"*Niente,*" Julian dismissed. He raised himself up, sat on the edge of the chair, and looked out over the water. He glanced at his phone to check messages.

As the other man rearranged his table, he asked where Julian was from, "*Di dove è?*"

"Atlanta," Julian replied. *E Lei?*

The man's eyes widened. He hadn't expected Atlanta. "*Vengo da Milano.* Where did you learn to speak Italian?"

"Here and there."

"Ah," the man murmured. "It's good."

Julian glanced at the man's book. It was a historical novel about Augustus. "How's the book?"

"I just started it. It seems good."

"He's a talented author. He tells a good story."

"You know him?"

"I know his work," Julian replied, although he knew the author in person.

"*Lorenzo,*" he said, reaching over to shake Julian's hand.

"*Julian. Piacere.*"

Lorenzo sat up and faced Julian. The server brought Julian his salad and wine. Julian said, "Would you like something to eat or drink?"

Lorenzo nodded and asked for a glass of wine. The server returned quickly with a glass for him. They toasted, "*Salute.*"

Lorenzo was probably about sixty. He was in good shape for his age. He was tall, lean, and dark – with short cropped dark hair. He had a warm smile and dark brown eyes.

"What brings you to Capri?" he asked Julian.

"This," Julian said with a chuckle, waving his hand over the deck and water.

"Ah, yes. It is magical," Lorenzo said, looking around.

"And you?"

"A break from Milan. Sometimes one needs a little sun and warmth."

Julian nodded.

"Are you here with your wife?" Julian asked, looking at his ring.

"God no," Lorenzo said excitedly. He hesitated and then said, "I'm not married."

Julian detected his hesitation and apologized. "I'm sorry. I shouldn't have presumed."

"It's okay. I get that all the time. I guess I should quit wearing the ring."

"Are you divorced, widowed?"

"Gay."

"Oh," Julian said. "Sorry again."

"Don't be."

Julian took a sip of wine and pushed a few leaves of lettuce around in his bowl. "Can I ask you something?" Julian began, looking down at his food.

"Sure," Lorenzo said.

"When did you know?"

Lorenzo was at first taken back by the direct question, but sensed that Julian might be struggling with coming out and said thoughtfully, "Well, for me, I knew early on. But for a lot of my friends, they only realized it later in life."

Julian looked up, intrigued. Lorenzo smiled. He then added, "I am lucky living in Milan where there's more openness. Other parts of Italy and the world are more difficult."

Julian nodded. Lorenzo took a sip of wine and gazed at Julian over the top of his glass. "And you? Wife?" he asked, looking at Julian's ring but certain there was no wife.

"Widower."

"*Mi dispiace.*"

"*Grazie.*"

"*E allora?*" Lorenzo asked Julian what might be next.

Julian rubbed his chin. Lorenzo seemed genuinely interested in continuing a conversation.

"I'm wondering," Julian began tentatively. Lorenzo nodded encouragingly. "I'm wondering if I might have overlooked something over the years."

"You mean, that maybe you might be gay?"

Julian nodded tentatively. It was a big step to even consider the idea.

"What's making you think that?"

"I met someone. I'm intrigued. I've begun to notice my own curiosity."

"So, what's the problem?" Lorenzo pressed, sensing there was something Julian was struggling with.

"First of all, how can you be married for 30 years, and not know?"

"I can't answer that personally, but I have friends who came out late, as I said earlier. Many had wives who were full of life and who filled a room. They were charming, sensual, affectionate, and fun. It's easy to get swept up in their lives or to get bogged down in the daily routine of work and parenting."

"And, what if you think you might be?"

Lorenzo looked out over the water and turned back to Julian. "You'll know. It will become more obvious and undeniable."

"In what sense?"

"Well, who you're attracted to, for one. What draws your eye, what you notice – men or women."

Julian nodded.

Lorenzo leaned forward and made a cautionary gesture with his hand. "I don't know you, and I shouldn't be giving advice. At some point you must experiment if you haven't already. But one thing I know is true – at this stage in your life – don't experiment with someone who you aren't passionate about. It's easy to get turned off by a bad trick." Lorenzo winked.

Julian looked off in the distance, not sure what the word trick meant. "What if you're attracted to someone but not sure about their orientation?"

"That's complicated," Lorenzo said, shaking his head. "If he's gay and you connect with each other, it will work out. If he's not, and you become friends before that becomes obvious, you shouldn't have anything to fear."

Julian sighed and knew what he had to do.

Later that afternoon, Julian hired a small boat to take him to Marina Piccola, where he made his way up the hill to the villa. Bruno was already inside, cleaning brushes from his session.

"Can I see what you did?" Julian asked enthusiastically.

Bruno nodded. He set down the brushes and walked across the room to a table. He lifted a canvas. "What do you think?"

"Wow!" Julian said. "You did that today?"

Bruno nodded proudly. He began to tear up, choked with emotion. With a trembling voice, he said, "It was incredible. It came so naturally. It was almost as if I wasn't looking at the scene – that I was painting something that was inside me, that was me."

"Tell me more."

"Remember yesterday when I said life is beautiful and rough?"

Julian nodded.

"I could see it in the tree clinging tenaciously to the crevasse hanging out over the cliff – beautiful and vulnerable yet somehow surviving wind, rain, and landslides. As I painted, I felt like I was painting me. I know that must sound silly, but it's true."

"No. It doesn't. I can see it in your face and sense it in your voice."

Julian detected a peace and serenity in Bruno as he spoke. He wanted to reach over to him and give him an embrace, but he held back. "Did you notice any other things you'd like to paint tomorrow?"

"I was wondering if you might like to explore with me tomorrow," Bruno asked.

"I don't want to distract from your focus or concentration," Julian said thoughtfully.

"Do you think I'll be distracted with you around?" Bruno said playfully.

"Depends on where we go and what we're wearing," Julian said, wishing he had dialed it back and notch and not been so forward.

Bruno smiled broadly, and a dimple formed at the corner of his mouth. It was a playful and boyish grin. "Professor, I'm shocked at your insinuation."

"And I'm shocked that your sensitivities are so aroused."

Now it was time for Bruno to overstate, "It's not my sensitivities that are aroused."

"Wow!" Julian said, "I wasn't expecting that."

"Me, either!" Bruno chuckled, holding his hand up to his mouth.

"We need a drink," Julian suggested.

"Let me finish here, and I'll come up."

Julian nodded, went upstairs, and opened some wine. Bruno joined him shortly, and they sat on the balcony looking out over the sea that was picking up the early evening hues of pink and purple in the sky.

"And what did you do today?" Bruno asked Julian, raising his glass in a toast.

"I ran to the Faraglioni where I laid on the terrace, swam, and had a little lunch. It is so beautiful there."

"You'll have to take me."

"And dinner tonight? What should we do?" Julian asked.

"Marianna had some things stocked in the fridge. Let's take a look. I wouldn't mind making some pasta – perhaps something simple, tomatoes, basil, and a salad."

"Sounds good to me," Julian said.

They finished their drinks and went into the kitchen and found the ingredients for a simple but tasty dinner. The glass doors were open in the dining room, and a gentle breeze blew up the hillside, filling the room with the scent of sea air. Bruno lit some candles, and they ate as the sun set and the sky became a dark indigo color.

Julian's dark wavy hair rustled in the breeze, and the flicker of golden candlelight illuminated his face. "You're very handsome, you know," Bruno said tenderly.

Julian wasn't expecting that, and blushed. It dispelled fears that Bruno didn't find him attractive. Encouraged, he said, "You're handsome yourself. I noticed you the first day."

Bruno grinned. He felt like Julian was dropping clues he was comfortable looking at men. After a pause, he asked, "By the way, in Rome, are you staying with friends or in a vacation rental? That's a unique location you're at."

"Family friends," Julian said misleadingly. "Now, back to you," he continued. "Most artists are a little gritty. You're very polished. You take care of yourself."

"I think I picked that up from my parents. They dressed well. My mother was very stylish, and my father worked out – even as he got older."

"I bet you were a hottie in school."

"Was?" Bruno asked.

Julian didn't know how to respond without saying Bruno was hot now, and that seemed too forward. He just winked.

They had finished dinner, and Bruno picked up their plates and walked to the kitchen. "Espresso?"

Julian nodded.

Bruno came back out, placed one hand on Julian's shoulder, and set the espresso cup down in front of him. Julian felt the charge of energy rush through his shoulder and across his chest. He couldn't believe how such a simple gesture could be so potent. He glanced up at Bruno, who smiled and took his seat across from Julian.

They drank their coffee, and Bruno poured them each a glass of brandy.

"Can I ask you something?" Bruno began carefully, thoughtfully.

Julian nodded.

"Yesterday, by the pool. What was that?"

Julian shuffled nervously in his chair. He then said, "I'm sorry. I crossed a line. I don't know what came over me. Curiosity, need, anger, resentment."

"Anger and resentment?" Bruno stated with his forehead creased.

"Anger at my wife, resentment toward her."

"And curiosity?"

"I don't know. I guess I'm curious. What would it be like to do it with a man?"

"I'm curious, too," Bruno said, pretending innocence and inexperience. He sighed to imply anxiousness.

Julian's eyes widened, and he raised one of his brows inquisitively.

"It felt rather natural, I have to say," Julian said.

Continuing his narrative, Bruno said, "I imagine that since we are the same sex, we know how things work and what turns a man on. There's very little learning curve, at least that's what I imagine."

Julian nodded. "That makes sense." He looked off to the side of the room, focusing on a large decorative platter hung on the wall. Turning back to Bruno, he continued, "I like you – as a friend. I would hate to spoil that."

"Me, too," Bruno added.

They finished their drinks, continuing to chat and learn more about each other. As it got later, Julian said, "I think I need to turn in. I'm pretty tired from the day."

"Me, too. Will you come with me tomorrow?"

"Sure."

They embraced and kissed each other on the cheek. Julian walked down the hall to his room, stripped off his shorts and tee-shirt, washed up in the bathroom, and slipped under the covers. He laid on his back, looking up at the ceiling. He thought of Bruno, just down the hall, lying naked in his own bed. He wished he could sleep with him, and he wondered if Bruno felt the same way.

Bruno laid on his stomach, clutching two pillows close to him. He ached for Julian, and every fiber of his body wanted to walk down the hall and make passionate love to him. He was now convinced Julian was comfortable, but he didn't want to come on too strong, nor did he want to break the spell they were under.

Both tossed and turned, each wishing the other would take the initiative and search the other one out. Bruno managed a little sleep and Julian finally tired of his thoughts enough to close his eyes and doze off.

Morning came early. They both put on shorts and met in the kitchen, preparing several large double espressos. Julian looked at Bruno, who looked like he had a hangover, except they hadn't drunk enough for hangovers. Bruno noticed the bags under Julian's eyes and wondered if he had suffered the same restless night as he.

After showering, Bruno went into Julian's room and said, "Will you come with me today?"

"Sure. I'd love to. Where?"

"There are some paths along the shore. I'm hoping I might find some other settings that work."

"Ready to go?"

Bruno nodded.

They headed toward the Faraglioni and then beyond the restaurant and terrace to a series of primitive trails that ran just above the water's edge. The scenery was breathtaking. Rocky hillsides covered in brush plunged into the sea with ethereal views of the peninsula of Sorrento off into the distance. Bruno was having a hard time finding another setting for a composition. They were tired from the hike and decided to take a break. They were on a path just feet above the water in a secluded cove.

"Care for a swim?" Bruno asked Julian.

"Yes. It's getting warm."

Bruno unbuttoned his shirt, slipped off his shoes, and then dropped his shorts. He leaped into the water, swimming a few strokes away from the shore. Julian followed suit, pulling off his tee-shirt and dropping his shorts as well. He leaped in and swam up to Bruno. Without hesitation, he approached Bruno and gave him a kiss.

Bruno tilted his head back and looked inquisitively at Julian. Julian maintained his proximity to Bruno, their cocks brushing each other as they bobbed in the water. "Hey cutie," Julian said tenderly with a sheepish grin.

Bruno just smiled warmly. He stared into Julian's eyes and knew he was smitten and hopelessly lost. "*Dio mio,*" he murmured to himself. "*Sono perduto.*"

Julian reached his legs around Bruno and pulled himself close, his increasingly hard cock pressed against Bruno's taut abdomen. Bruno's long shaft searched for the space between Julian's buttocks. Julian closed his eyes as he felt Bruno under him.

They were in deep water and moved closer to shore. Julian looked nervously around, but it was clear they were in a remote place. The shoreline was rocky, but just under the surface of the water, a few smooth boulders created a comfortable ledge where they sat.

Julian reached over and pulled Bruno's head close to his and gave him a deep kiss. Bruno tasted earthy and salty – it was intoxicating. Bruno ran his hand over Julian's side and thighs, brushing his erection and rubbing the glans which shined in the sun. Julian arched his back as Bruno stroked him.

"*Non ci posso credere,*" Bruno whispered. It was a fantasy come true – making love to a man who was more than a quick trick. It was unfamiliar territory, and he was more disoriented than he had ever expected.

Julian seemed to know exactly what to do. He grabbed hold of Bruno and turned him toward him, letting the buoyancy of the saltwater lift him over his shaft. He found the deep crevasse of Bruno's butt, and pressed firmly, the saltwater forming a slippery lubricant. Bruno relaxed and let Julian in. Julian took hold of Bruno's large cock and stroked it in rhythm with his own thrusts. Julian opened his mouth around Bruno's and kissed him deeply. They both felt a weightless buoyancy as the water lapped against their bodies and they breathed each other in. There was no longer a demarcation between one body and the other, between their bodies and the water, between the water, and the light, and the air. Julian felt his skin tighten as he felt waves of pleasure rise within him. He let go of Bruno's mouth and leaned down, running his mouth around the hard edge of Bruno's sculpted pecs. He tugged playfully on his nipples and felt Bruno's cock throb in anticipation.

They both felt pulsations rising within their bodies and gazed into each other's eyes. For both, it was the first time making love with eyes open. Julian noticed Bruno's widening as waves of pleasure continued to mount. Bruno, in turn, peered into Julian's eyes – intense, affectionate, and full of longing.

They both exploded in spasms of release, Julian throbbing inside Bruno and Bruno's load, breaching the surface of the water with a powerful thrust.

"Oh my God," Julian exclaimed, pulling out of Bruno and resting his head on Bruno's shoulder.

Bruno wrapped his arms around Julian and said, "*Quanto sei bello!*"

Bruno eventually let go of Julian and pushed off into deeper water, letting the saltwater rinse away their exchange. Julian swam toward him and treaded nearby.

Both were at a loss for words, neither wanting to break the spell. Eventually Bruno said, "I'm not sure I'm up for a painting session. Shall we head back?"

"I told you I would be a distraction," Julian joked. "I know a nice place to get something to eat – near the Faraglioni. You up for it?"

"We're not dressed."

"During the day, everyone is in bathing suits. We'll fit in fine. We can get something at the bar."

They dried in the sun, dressed, and walked toward the restaurant. Both were quiet, but it was not an awkward silence. Rather, they were content and in awe of what they had just shared.

They found two seats at the bar and ordered wine and salads. Bruno gazed at the amazing views of the Faraglioni, and Julian scanned the terrace to see if he might see Lorenzo. Off in the corner, he was reading his book about Augustus. He glanced up, noticed Julian, and winked.

"This is magnificent," Bruno remarked as the bartender poured him a glass of cold white wine. He glanced up and down the bar at the gathering of well-heeled clientele.

An Italian couple leaned over and asked, "Aren't you Bruno Muzzi?"

He nodded nervously.

"We don't want to disturb you, but we love your work. We met you at one of your exhibitions. We have one of your paintings of the Forum."

"Thank you," he said warmly. "Are you from Rome?"

They nodded and glanced over at Julian. Bruno noticed. He said, "This is my friend Julian, a classics professor."

"*Sono Enrico e questa è Maria.*"

"*Piacere. Julian Phillips.*"

"Where do you teach?" Enrico asked.

"In Atlanta."

Surprised, Enrico said, "And what brings you to Italy?"

"Research."

"Julian is being modest. He's translating a newly found codex from Ostia for the Capitoline Museums."

"Wow! How exciting," Maria noted.

Julian wanted to say, 'yes, but not as exciting as what I just did with Bruno,' but he checked his errant thoughts and said, "Yes, it's very exciting. I hope it will add new perspectives to our understanding of late Roman civilization."

Everyone continued to chat until lunches arrived. The bartender refilled Bruno's and Julian's glasses, and they dug into the spaghetti alle vongole. The clams were substantial, and the flavors were perfectly balanced with garlic, lemon, and oil.

Bruno was surprised that he was recognized and was relieved that he could introduce Julian as a professor, someone with whom a painter of classic Roman sites might know as a colleague or friend.

It was better than people thinking they were two middle-aged men having an affair.

Julian kept looking over at Lorenzo at the edge of the terrace. Lorenzo stood and walked toward the bar, ordering a drink across from Julian and Bruno. Julian caught his eye. Lorenzo nodded.

"Do you know him?" Bruno inquired, noticing their eye contact.

"We met briefly the other day when I was here for lunch," Julian replied.

Bruno's gaydar went off, and he became alarmed. He stared at Lorenzo, who was experienced enough to know when someone was staring him down. He walked over to Julian and Bruno and said, "I believe we met the other day." He extended his hands to Julian.

"*Sì, sono Julian. E questo è Bruno.*"

"*Piacere. Lorenzo.*"

"Lorenzo sat near me the other day, and we had a pleasant conversation about Augustus," Julian said, trying to establish a narrative that wouldn't alarm Bruno.

"Ah, yes, Julian said he enjoyed himself here the other day," Bruno said pointedly.

"It's a magnificent spot for swimming, eating, relaxing," Lorenzo added, looking up and down Julian's torso.

Julian watched Bruno's face become tense. He ended the conversation preemptively. "It was nice to see you again. Hope you have a nice day."

Lorenzo was taken aback by Julian's quick ending of the conversation, but could understand why and said, "Yes. Nice to run into you again. Hope you guys have a nice time."

Bruno was experienced enough to know when a conversation was riddled with sexual tension and wondered if Julian wasn't hiding something. As Lorenzo walked away, Bruno asked, "So, you met him the other day?"

"Yes. Briefly. He was seated near me on the terrace."

"And you talked about Augustus?" Bruno asked incredulously.

"Yes. He was reading a novel about him. I knew the author."

"Ah. Curious."

Julian felt Bruno's territorial questions and shifted subjects, saying, "After lunch, should we head back to the villa, or do you want to stay here and swim?"

"I would like to go back. I have some work I'd like to do on the painting from yesterday," he said curtly.

"Yes. I could probably do some work on my computer as well."

They nodded to each other, finished their spaghetti with clams, and headed back to the villa. The walk was quiet and filled with tension. Julian could feel Bruno's uneasiness and interpreted it as his discomfort with their sexual exchange earlier. He also wondered if Bruno had picked up on Lorenzo's orientation and was having second thoughts about whether he belonged to that tribe or not.

Bruno was feeling vulnerable for having given in to his feelings for Julian and realized Julian was a head turner. He worried he would have to fight for him, and that brought up old wounds, wounds he had nursed for decades.

Both were wondering what the next step might be. They walked into the villa, went into separate bathrooms to pee, and came back out into the hallway. Despite the tension, Julian found Bruno irresistible and walked up to him and gave him a warm kiss. Bruno melted, unable to contain his affection for Julian.

"Is it time for a siesta?" Bruno asked with a grin.

"Yeah. I think the wine and pasta are setting in," Julian said without being too forward. He wanted Bruno to take his hand and lead him to his bed. Bruno must have read his mind. He took Julian's hand and silently led him into his bedroom.

He lifted Julian's tee-shirt up over his shoulders and leaned down, kissing his smooth pecs. Julian became instantly aroused and said, "I thought we were going to take a nap."

"I'm getting you ready for bed," Bruno whispered.

Julian looked around. He sat on the edge of the bed, and Bruno sat down next to him. He seemed deep in thought, and Julian wondered if he was still reticent. Julian rubbed his hands over Bruno's thighs and slid them up into the folds of his shorts. He could tell Bruno was aroused, but he seemed hesitant to reciprocate. He felt increasingly perplexed that Bruno would come on strong and then hesitate, pull back. He decided to take a softer approach. He reached his arm around Bruno and pulled him down next to him on the bed, spooning him and holding him tenderly.

Bruno closed his eyes and, for a moment, relaxed in Julian's embrace. Trusting someone was so alien. He took several deep breaths, hoping he could quiet his racing heart. The words of Marianna echoed in his head. "Love requires us to be vulnerable. It's been thirty years. Give it a try."

Bruno rolled around and faced Julian, nuzzling his nose into Julian's chest. His firm, smooth skin was sensual and arousing, and he said, "Ti voglio bene."

Julian gasped. He hadn't expected such a bold declaration of love. He furrowed his forehead. Bruno interpreted it as a look of fear and apprehension, so he said, "Sorry. I must have lost myself."

"No. Don't apologize. I'm glad you feel that way. I thought I was coming on too strong."

Bruno kissed Julian and murmured, "No. That's not the problem. I've been burned before. I guess I'm nervous."

Julian found it difficult to believe Bruno would be nervous. He seemed so self-confident, strong, in control of things. "I guess we're both nervous," Julian said thoughtfully.

Bruno nodded. He unbuttoned Julian's shorts and slid them off. He unbuttoned his own shirt and shorts and slipped them off. He laid next to Julian, wrapping his left arm over his back and nuzzling his hardness into Julian's side. Julian wrapped his arms around the fluffy pillow and made himself comfortable, savoring the physical intimacy of Bruno's body wrapped around his. In a low voice he said, "I love you, too."

Bruno smiled contently. 'Maybe he could become vulnerable again,' he thought to himself. He closed his eyes and listened to the soft breaths of Julian next to him. They both soon fell into a peaceful sleep.

12

Chapter Twelve – Secrets

"Who are these people we're meeting?" Bruno pressed as they headed to Luciana's apartment near the Via Giulia.

"Colleagues from work."

"So, they're all nerdy scholars, right?"

"Just like me," Julian said, with an irony lost on Bruno.

They reached Luciana's building, pressed the buzzer, and she let them in. They climbed the stairs. Luciana was at the stop of the stairs, waving them up. As they reached the landing, Luciana gave Julian a warm kiss on both cheeks and then looked warmly at Bruno.

"Luciana, this is Bruno. Bruno, Luciana, my colleague and friend from the Capitoline Museums."

She waved her hand dismissively. "I prefer Luciana from the Via Giulia or something like that."

"You're the artist Julian has been talking about," she said, raising one of her brows. "Delicious!"

"Come in. Let me get you something to drink. Wine?"

Julian and Bruno both nodded.

"What a nice place you have," Bruno began, noticing her unique artistic taste. "I see you like modern art."

"Afraid so. I spend so much time with classical pieces, it's nice to have a contrast at home."

She poured them both a glass of wine and lifted her glass. "*Salute!* And Welcome. Nice to meet you."

"The same. Julian has told me so much about you."

She glared at Julian, who smiled back. "The others will be here soon." Sofia walked in from the back of the apartment and smiled warmly at Julian.

"Julian. Welcome back." They exchanged kisses.

"Sofia, this is Bruno. Bruno, Sofia, Luciana's partner."

"*Piacere,*" they both said in unison.

Bruno whispered to Julian while Sofia and Luciana conferred about something, "Your colleague is a lesbian?"

Julian nodded. Bruno walked toward the perimeter of the parlor and examined Luciana's collection of art.

The buzzer rang, and shortly thereafter, Luca entered with a friend. Luca gave kisses to Luciana and introduced her to Giorgio. Luciana got them drinks and brought them into the parlor where Bruno, Julian and Sofia were discussing art.

Bruno turned toward Luciana as she was bringing Luca and Giorgio into the center of the room. When he saw Luca, he became ashen white. Luca's eyes widened as he recognized Bruno. Their expressions weren't lost on Luciana, who said, "Do you guys know each other?"

"Yes," Bruno began. "Rome is a small town."

"Indeed," Luca added. "Bruno, it's been a while." They air kissed coldly.

"Julian, nice to see you again," Luca began. "This is Giorgio. Giorgio, Julian and Bruno."

"*Piacere,*" Julian and Giorgio said.

"How's your work going?" Luca said to Julian, trying to contain the trembling he felt at having run into Bruno.

"Good. I'm making headway on the codex. And your work?"

"It's fine. We're in the busy tourist season, so there are extra things to do here and there."

The buzzer rang again, and Stefano walked in with Anna and Laura. Luciana got them drinks, and they gathered in the parlor with the rest, making introductions. Stefano kept looking at Bruno as if he knew him but couldn't quite place him. They spoke about art and local politics, but Stefano wasn't paying attention; he was struggling to put a memory on a face.

He and Luca walked over to the side of the room and talked alone with each other. Julian and Bruno were standing with Sofia, who was describing a recent trip to Turkey. Julian glanced over and noticed Stefano gazing at Bruno and nodding his head as Luca spoke. He was a little unnerved and walked toward them.

"Stefano, it's good to see you again," Julian began.

Stefano nodded. "I hear you've been busy," he began, looking at Luca.

Julian nodded. "The work has been engaging, and I've had a lot to do settling my wife's estate."

"Looks like you've been busy in other ways," Stefano added, glancing toward Bruno and winking.

"A surprise," Julian said simply.

"I bet," Luca said, trying to conceal his disdain.

They continued small talk. Julian and Bruno rejoined each other at the side of the room. Bruno said, "I may need to cut out early. I'm not feeling so well, and I have a busy day tomorrow."

"Anything the matter?"

"No. I think I might have gotten too much sun painting this morning. That's all. Nothing to be alarmed about, but I don't feel up to partying late."

"I understand. Let me know when you're ready to go, and I'll walk you out. You don't mind if I stay?"

Bruno shook his head. He remained a bit longer, hiding his face behind his glass as he drank heavily. Eventually, he nodded to Julian that he was ready to leave. He thanked Luciana for her hospitality and waved to the rest as he walked out the door. Luciana approached Julian and said, "Is everything okay?"

"Yes. He just wasn't feeling well."

Luca glared at Luciana, who excused herself and walked toward him, leaving Julian to chat with Sofia.

"Luciana, do you know who Julian's friend is?" he began immediately.

"He's an artist."

"Yes. He's Bruno Muzzi. He's famous for his ancient Roman pieces."

"Wow! I didn't know," she said.

"And, he has a reputation."

"A good one, I presume," she said.

Luca shook his head. "As an artist, yes, but he has a terrible reputation in the gay community."

Her eyes widened, and she placed her hand on his forearm. "Continue."

"He's very handsome and well-endowed," he began.

"That's obvious. Even I noticed."

"And he loves them and leaves them."

Luciana looked like she didn't understand, although Luca knew she was anything but naïve.

"He hooks up with guys but drops them once he's finished. There is a string of broken hearts across Rome. I'm one of them."

"You slept with Bruno?"

"Hmm hum."

"And?"

"He comes on very strong. He has an allure to him that is irresistible. He's affectionate and thoughtful but, once you get close, he finds some pretext for why the relationship isn't right, and leaves. That's if you get beyond a one-nighter. There are a lot of guys he just tricks with."

"Oh shit!" she said in alarm, her hand held up to her mouth. "This is not good for Julian."

"No. It's not. If he's just coming out, this is not a good first relationship or experience."

"I've got to find a way to warn him. Thanks for letting me know."

She extracted herself from Luca and circulated amongst the guests. Stefano stopped her and repeated what Luca had said and added, "Only with me, it was a one-night stand. He was charming and handsome. I couldn't believe my luck when he approached me at a discreet bar I frequent. I took him to my place. We had some of the best sex I've ever had, and I thought we had connected. He never called me back, and when I saw him on the street a week later, he acted as if we hadn't met. It was horrible."

Luciana wasn't surprised. She had similar experiences with straight married men who enjoyed her company and companionship but felt guilty for cheating on their wives and would ignore her on the street. "Men are pigs," she exclaimed to Stefano, who was taken aback. "Sorry. I don't mean you."

He sighed.

"How do we say something to Julian," Stefano pressed her as Luca approached.

"Are you all talking about Bruno?"

They both nodded.

"I'll figure out a way to talk to Julian. I have a pretext with our work. I'll have him come by the office tomorrow," Luciana said.

The next day, Luciana texted Julian and asked if he might come by the archives for a quick conferral around the codex. Julian arrived late morning, presented his credentials, and made his way to Luciana's office.

"Ah, Julian. You look nice!"

"And you, Luciana." They kissed. "Great party, by the way. Thanks for inviting us."

"Yes. It was nice. I'm glad you could come."

"You said you had something to show me," he began.

"Yes. She walked toward the hermetically sealed room, opened the door, and led them toward the codex. She had come up with a technical question she wanted to ask Julian. They discussed some issues with the original manuscript and the text, and Julian took some notes. They left the room and went back into her office.

"So, you and Bruno seem to be hitting it off nicely."

"Yes. What a surprise. I can see how someone can totally change your perspective – like you and Sofia."

Luciana nodded.

"Julian. I have something to share with you," she began anxiously.

He looked alarmed.

"Luca and Stefano know Bruno."

Julian creased his forehead, encouraging her to continue.

"Bruno has been around the block a few times."

"What do you mean?" Julian asked, already knowing the answer.

"Well, apparently he sleeps around a lot. Has sex with a lot of men and, if anyone gets close, he drops them."

"But that's not possible," Julian began. "He's struggling to accept his own orientation. We talked about how reticent he was."

"Well, that's not what Luca and Stefano have observed, first-hand."

Julian looked down and rubbed his chin. "I still don't believe it given what he shared with me."

"You have to be careful with Italian men," Luciana continued.

"Maybe they're no different from men anywhere. They'll tell you what they know you want to hear, enjoy you, and then they are off."

Julian realized Luciana was probably speaking from a good deal of experience, but he still found it difficult to believe that Bruno would have been so deceptive. "Are you sure Luca and Stefano aren't mistaken?"

"No, I'm not. But they have no reason to lie or fabricate a story," she said, placing her hand on Julian's forearm. "Maybe you just need to watch out, take notes, ask a lot of questions. Things could be okay, but just be careful."

Julian nodded.

Luciana added, "By the way, I'm surprised. I was only kidding with you a couple of weeks ago about switching sides. I didn't think you'd take me seriously. What happened?"

"It was unexpected. Maybe something had been percolating under the surface for a long time, and with Marcella's death and my being in Rome, it became obvious."

Luciana nodded and smiled. "I want to be happy for you. Just be careful. You don't need your first experience to be a bad one."

"It's funny. You're the second person who has said that to me."

Luciana creased her forehead.

They continued their visit, made plans to get together again, and closed the codex. Luciana returned to her work, and Julian walked back to his apartment. He texted Bruno to follow up with him.

"*Ciao, bello.* How are you? I hope you're feeling better."

There was no immediate response. Julian assumed Bruno was off painting. He took a walk to see if he might run into him. He made a big loop of major archaeological sites in the center, but Bruno was nowhere to be found. He returned home, did some reading, and fixed dinner. He was becoming more alarmed that he hadn't heard from Bruno and called him. He got his voicemail and left a message.

The next morning, he still hadn't heard from Bruno. He became increasingly worried that what Luciana had said was true, and he was being dumped, or Bruno was ill and needed attention. He went to his apartment. He rang the bell. There was no answer. A neighbor, out walking her dog, noticed Julian and said, "He went out painting earlier. You might try him this afternoon."

Julian thanked her and felt a twisting knot in his stomach. "*Cazzo!* I should have known."

He sent one more text: "Bruno. We need to talk."

13

Chapter Thirteen – More Secrets

"Marianna, I need to talk to you. Call me back," Bruno said, leaving a message on her phone.

Marianna called back shortly. "Bruno, what's the matter. You sound horrible."

"I am. I fucked things up."

"*Tesoro*, I've never heard you talk like this. What happened?"

"It's Julian. I'm such a shithead."

"Slow down. Are you free now? Let's meet for coffee. I am supposed to meet Gabriella at the gallery later. Why don't you meet me at that little café nearby?"

"Perfect. *A dopo*."

A half hour later, Bruno approached Marianna seated at a small table in the narrow side street near the Via Margutta. She could see the alarm on Bruno's face. She stood and embraced him warmly. "Sit. Tell me what happened."

"After Julian and I got back from Capri, which was incredible, we went to a party at his colleague's house. A couple of guys I've slept with were there. Oh, it was horrible."

"*Caro*, at your age – and at Julian's – you have to have had a history. One can't expect you to be a virgin. I'm sure he understands that."

"You don't understand. Luca and Stefano are only the tip of the iceberg."

"So, you've been around a bit. What's wrong with that?"

"I've been around a lot."

Marianna's face changed. She looked worried. She didn't know what to say.

"I'm sure he will understand if he loves you."

"I don't think so. I convinced him I was just beginning to accept my orientation – that I was curious even though I liked woman."

"So?"

"Once he finds out I have a reputation, he'll realize I was dishonest. Since he's just coming out, he'll be hurt and scared as shit."

"Bruno. I've known you for a long time. Let me say something – but hear me out and don't get upset."

Bruno nodded.

"As I said the other day, you have to let the demon of your father go, and you have to let go of the hurt you felt when what's her name treated you so badly. What was her name, again?"

"Marcella."

"Yes. Marcella."

"I'm trying to let all of that go."

"Exactly. That's good. That's growth. I'm proud of you, and if Julian knew the complete story, he would be understanding."

"I'm not so sure of that."

"Why not try to explain it to him?"

Bruno's face relaxed a bit, and he sighed deeply.

"Exactly. You need to take a deep breath and call him. Tell him you want to talk."

"I don't know. He's going to be really upset."

"You don't know that." Marianna looked at her watch and continued, "Come. Let's go see Gabriella. I have an appointment. She'll brighten you up."

Bruno nodded. They paid their tab and walked the short distance to the gallery.

Gabriella was dressed for an opening she was hosting later that evening. She was in tall leather boots, a short skirt, a low cut loose top, and her hair included stunning highlights. "Bruno! What a surprise."

Bruno kissed her on her cheeks. "I was having coffee with Marianna, and she said she was meeting you. I wanted to touch base with you anyway about the pieces I have ready."

Gabriella kissed Marianna and then turned back to Bruno. "Why so sullen?"

Marianna interjected, "Boy troubles."

"Tell me something new," Gabriella said playfully. She noticed Bruno didn't laugh or smile.

Marianna continued, "Real boy troubles. Love troubles."

"Love. I don't hear that word often in the same sentence as Bruno Muzzi. Is it a he or she?" she asked with a grin.

Bruno murmured, "He."

"Name?"

"Julian."

"So, you fell in love with this Julian? What's the problem?"

"He's afraid his reputation will haunt him and sabotage the relationship," Marianna commented.

"So, you're actually thinking this might be a long-term relationship? Now you have me intrigued."

Bruno nodded. "He's different. We've connected at a deep level. He's so handsome and talented."

"Apparently, he's a scholar from the States," Marianna added.

Gabriella gasped. "You said his name is Julian? He's from the States? What's his last name?"

"I don't know. I just know him as Julian. I think he has a typical American or English sounding name – something like Phillips. Yes, I think that's it."

"Oh my God!" Gabriella exclaimed.

Marianna and Bruno both looked at each other. "What's the matter?" Marianna pressed.

"Do you know where he lives?" Gabriella inquired.

"I haven't been to his place, but he spotted me first from his window overlooking Trajan's Forum."

"Oh my God!" Gabriella exclaimed again. "Julian is married to Marcella."

"My Marcella?" Bruno said.

Gabriella nodded. Then, choking with emotion, she said, "And Marcella just passed."

Bruno got dizzy. Marianna noticed and dragged a chair from behind the desk. "Sit."

He didn't protest. Gabriella handed him a bottle of water.

"Marcella passed? How?"

"Apparently of breast cancer. It's so sad," Gabriella continued.

"How do you know this?" Bruno inquired, perplexed.

"Julian came into the gallery a few weeks ago. He had your card and wanted to see your work. He wanted to be put on the contact list for the show in September. When he told me his name, I couldn't believe it. When he told me she had just died, I was heartbroken. She and I had been friends in school."

"What are the chances?" Marianna murmured, shaking her head.

Bruno nodded. He sobbed. "*Dio mio*, this can't be happening."

Marianna rubbed her hand on his shoulder. "Let me take you home. We need to get you to lie down on a sofa." She glanced at Gabriella in alarm.

Gabriella nodded and called for a taxi. A half-hour later, Marianna led Bruno into his apartment, turned on a few lights, and led him to the large sofa where she helped him lay down. She got a blanket and covered him. She put on some water and prepared tea.

"*Cazzo*, this changes everything," Bruno began excitedly as he took a few sips from the steaming cup. He was sitting up, a blanket draped over his shoulders.

"How so?" Marianna pressed.

"He stole her from me. He stole my life."

"That was a long time ago. I'm sure there's an explanation."

"Even if there was, I'm not sure I could be with him. I would keep seeing her. It's too much."

Marianna nodded thoughtfully. "Yes. I can see that would be a problem."

"Marcella and I were so in love. Suddenly, she's calling it off and moving to the States. She must have been having an affair."

Marianna looked off into the distance. "I know it's painful, dear, but were there any clues before she left, problems you might have been having?"

"No," he said emphatically.

"Do you think she suspected?"

"Suspected what?"

"That you're queer?"

"I'm not queer. I'm fluid."

"Okay, whatever. Did she suspect you played on both teams?"

"No. In fact, at the time, I didn't."

"So, no other issues at the time? Fights? Disputes?"

"Her father didn't like me."

"Ah, well, that's an important piece of information you left out.

Marcella's father was a force to be reckoned with. Maybe he gave her an ultimatum."

Bruno looked intrigued.

"And don't you think it's more than coincidental that Marcella's two loves were both gay?"

"I'm not gay."

"Honey. I still think you need to open that closet door."

"What if Marcella was drawn to men who allowed her to keep a certain emotional distance? Maybe she was protecting herself. We don't know what people have been through and what pain they carry inside," Marianna added.

Bruno took a deep breath as he realized he had been carrying around a lot of hurt himself. "Nevertheless, I could never be with Julian. It would be too weird."

Marianna looked off into the distance in thought. "Yes, it's certainly weird. But your meeting is extraordinarily unlikely and, for that reason, probably profoundly meaningful."

"In what sense?"

"Well, perhaps that you were destined to meet."

"You mean as in soulmates? You know I don't buy into that stuff."

"I didn't say it. It's just what are the chances?"

Bruno seemed deep in thought and began another line of questioning. "What about my past? I'm embarrassed, and if I were Julian, I'd run for the hills."

"Maybe you can explain, and he will understand."

"What's he going to understand? That I'm a sex addict."

"Is that who you think you are?"

Bruno nodded.

"Let me give you some armchair psychological insight. You're not an addict. You're acting out a deep trauma. What Marcella did to you was unforgivable, and it's not surprising that you would keep people at arm's length to avoid getting hurt again. I've watched you over the years. I never judged you for the string of broken hearts you left across Rome. I felt sorry for the hurt that drove that."

He nodded as if what Marianna said made sense. "What should I do?"

"I would call Julian and tell him you want to talk. Get it all out in the open. Explain what happened. If you are meant to be with each other, he will understand, and it will work out."

"You think so?" Bruno said with a glimmer of hope in his eyes.

Marianna nodded.

14

Chapter Fourteen –
Second Thoughts

It had been four days since Julian and Bruno returned from Capri, and three days since Luciana's party, and the deafening silence from Bruno. Julian poured himself into his work, racing through the codex at a record pace. He thought he might be able to finish the initial translation in a week or two and then head back to Atlanta to do the commentary before the school year began.

"*Il signor Alberti, per favore*," he said, as the receptionist at the law firm answered the phone.

"*Chi parla?*" she asked

"Tell him it's Julian Phillips. I need to confer with him."

"*Un attimo*," she said as she put him on hold.

A few moments later, Mr. Alberti came on the line. "Julian. What a pleasure. How are things going?"

"Everything is good. However, I'm beginning to think I would like to sell the residence to Piero's niece, if she is still interested. It's too big a responsibility for me to take on, and I plan on returning to the States in the Fall to teach."

"Are you sure? It's only been a short while since Marcella passed. Maybe you should give it some time."

"I've given it thought, and I'm ready to cut the cord."

"*Mi dispiace*. It would have been nice to have you remain in Rome. I had some contacts at the Sapienza who have always mentioned interest in having you to teach here, even if for a semester or two."

"I love Rome. But the residence is laden with Marcella's family's presence, and I need to move on."

"Whatever you say, Dr. Phillips. I'll reach out to the niece and see what she has in mind."

"Thank you."

Julian returned home and opened his computer and pulled up the electronic files of the codex. He found the place where he had left off and began to work on the text. Bruno's card laid on the edge of the table. He felt it glaring at him. He picked it up, crumbled it in his hand, and tossed it in a small trashcan nearby. "Fuck!" he said with uncharacteristic intensity. "How could I have been so naïve?"

He glanced over at the photograph of Marcella and her parents. She seemed so full of life that I couldn't believe that she could have succumbed to cancer.

"Maybe it's for the best," he murmured to himself. "Nothing is holding me here. I can finish my work, return to Atlanta, and pick up anew. I have my daughters to worry about, and I have a nice circle of colleagues at the university."

In the codex, Aurelius wrote about his wife's work as a deaconess. He was proud of her. Most wives in his class did little but remain at home and attend social gatherings. Adora tended to the sick, helped provide care for new immigrants, and distributed food and clothing and other goods to the poor.

They spent less time together. He remained in Ostia to oversee their business, and Adora remained at their residence in Rome, sometimes hosting local Christian suppers. They called them 'agape' meals. He thought the use of the Greek term for love pretentious, but she liked her work and community, and it kept her busy.

Aurelius loved his wife, but he was alarmed at what he perceived to be a poison pill in the new religion. Their leader, Jesus, taught people to love one another. This drew Adora to the religion, and she lived it out. But the religion argued that there is only one God. While there was some philosophical basis for the idea of a unified divine reality, and Aurelius was intrigued by that, he was upset by how leaders were using monotheism to consolidate power. He noticed an increased intolerance for diversity. He noted that Adora and her circle were growing hostile to Aurelius and his family traditions.

As Julian continued to read the codex, a passage jumped out at him. Aurelius mentioned a friend, Felix, who had lost his wife. They spent more time together in the absence of Adora. Aurelius didn't mince words regarding his affection for Felix and the consolation he felt when they gathered for a meal or time at the baths. Nevertheless, Julian picked up on an underlying or latent sadness in Aurelius's reflections.

Julian felt empathy for Aurelius and could relate given the sadness he felt over Marcella's death and now the disappointment over Bruno. He wanted to return to the comfort of his home and to the culture and traditions that were native to him. And, although the affection and intimacy with Bruno had been exciting, perhaps that, too, needed to be set aside.

He made a few notations on his computer and closed it shut. As he was about to get up and make some lunch, he received a text from Bruno: "Julian. Can we talk?"

15

Chapter Fifteen – Confessions

Julian sat across from Bruno at a small wine bar. It was early evening. The sun was low on the horizon, and patio lights had just come on, casting an orange glow on their faces. Both were pensive, quiet, sullen.

"I'm sorry I didn't respond to your calls or texts," Bruno began.

"I was worried," Julian replied without elaboration.

"I was embarrassed."

"Why?"

"I imagine Luca, or Stefano, or Luciana must have shared information with you about me."

"They may have mentioned a few things," Julian said without emotion, giving Bruno a stern look.

Bruno's head hung low, and he nervously fussed with his napkin. He took a long sip of his wine.

"I need to explain. I am a little more experienced with men than I might have led you to believe."

Julian nodded.

"I have a problem."

A look of alarm raced across Julian's face. He nodded for Bruno to continue.

"In college, I became engaged to a woman to get married. She was beautiful. We shared lots of common interests – art, history, travel, food. We were madly in love with each other."

"And?"

"One day, she told me she was breaking up. The engagement was over."

"Suddenly? Out of the blue?"

Bruno nodded. "She said she wasn't ready to marry, that she needed more time. She wanted to finish her graduate studies."

"You're kidding. You don't think she was having an affair or something?"

"That's what I thought, but I never uncovered anything except that she married soon afterwards. She must have been seeing someone."

"No clues in advance?"

"None. I couldn't believe someone could be so in love and then suddenly they aren't."

"You said you've been with a lot of men?"

Bruno nodded solemnly. "After we separated, I went into a dark place. I avoided people and poured myself into my art. They say a lot of creativity is inspired by pain, and it was certainly the case with me."

"And men?"

"I supposed I had a visceral negative reaction to women at first. I hung out with my male friends. I went on a trip with one. I didn't realize he was gay. He came onto me. The touch and the sex felt good. I was surprised."

"Then what happened?"

"At first I resisted. I tried to convince myself, I'm not gay. We didn't interact anymore. But I was curious and hooked up with someone in my neighborhood. It felt good to have sex without giving my heart. With men, I wasn't afraid I would fall in love. It was self-defense."

"That makes sense."

"But, at some point, you have to grow up. I didn't. To my surprise, I fell in love several times, with men, but I was so afraid to let go. I would always come up with a pretext for why it wasn't working."

"And?"

"Then I'd have a series of casual anonymous encounters until one of them tugged at my heart. I'd repeat the process."

"And me?"

"Well," Bruno began slowly, wringing his hands. "Then there was you."

Julian raised his brows.

Bruno continued, "You came out of nowhere, a phantom observer who showed up here and there as I worked. You were hot. I would pack up my paints, head home, and obsess over this guy – you – who seemed interested in my art, perhaps in me."

Julian seemed encouraged by the narrative Bruno was recounting. He relaxed his shoulders and breathed with more ease. He smiled.

Bruno noticed the smile and continued. "I presumed you were uneasy about sex with men, so I downplayed my past. I probably shouldn't have, but I didn't know what else to do. Then at the party, I ran into Luca and Stefano and realized my past would haunt me, catch up with me. I panicked and ran."

"We all have pasts," Julian said.

Bruno nodded. He waited to see if Julian might elaborate, might finally come clean about being a widower.

"Yes," he murmured quietly, "we have pasts."

"It sounds like you're still not over this woman who left you. Until you face that demon, you'll continue to second guess yourself and hold back."

Bruno nodded.

"What is her name? Where is she?"

Bruno sat quietly. He took a sip of wine to avoid eye contact with Julian, looking off in the distance as he placed the glass back down on the table. His body felt heavy, and all senses became inert – smell, sight, sound. Julian stared at Bruno, waiting for his answer. Bruno felt immobilized, frozen in place, not sure what to do or say. Julian reached over and touched the top of Bruno's hand, intuitively sensing that he was someplace else.

"Bruno. What's her name? Where is she?"

"Marcella."

16

Chapter Sixteen – Luna

Julian's bags were packed. He took one more walk around the apartment, slipped the photo of Marcella, Piero, and Camilla into his valise, and walked toward the door. He had called a taxi. As he walked down the marble staircase out onto the pavement overlooking Trajan's Forum, he noticed Bruno leaning against the taxi parked in front of the residence.

"Bruno?" he asked.

Bruno gazed at him, a look of tenderness, longing, and regret. "I couldn't let you leave without saying goodbye."

Julian felt the muscles in his chest tighten. He found Bruno irresistible, but an enigma he was unwilling to solve. It was all too complicated and strange, and he had made peace with his decision to return to Atlanta and sell the residence.

He felt embarrassed about not having shared information earlier with Bruno about being a widower and felt even worse knowing he was the direct cause of countless years of torment, having taken Marcella from him. Their conversation several nights earlier had been surreal – a cruel trick of destiny, two lives colliding with momentum and merciless force. Bruno longed to make sense of Marcella's sudden change of heart. Julian was stunned by the implausible likelihood of their having met. Both grappled with conflicting emotions of passion, hurt, and anger. Each walked away, unable to reconcile their feelings.

Now they stood facing each other.

"I'm sorry," Bruno began.

"Me, too," Julian added.

They stared at each other, each searching for an appropriate way to cross the barrier they faced.

"Your flight is this morning?"

"No. Later. I'm flying to Berlin this afternoon for a conference. I'm heading to the lawyers' office to sign papers for the sale of the residence."

"Don't," Bruno said unequivocally.

Julian creased his forehead and gazed at Bruno.

"Don't sell it. There's unfinished business here."

"I have to. Things are in motion. I have to move on."

"*Ti prego, no.* Let's talk."

"I'm sorry," Julian reiterated, stepping into the taxi. He shut the door. Bruno leaned on the window with an imploring face.

"*Dove?*" the driver asked.

Julian gave him Alberti's address in the Prati, and the driver sped off. Julian glanced back. Bruno placed his hands on his head in frustration and kicked the ground with his feet.

A few minutes later, the taxi pulled up to Alberti's office. Julian took the lift to the second floor and entered the posh suite of offices. The receptionist greeted him. "Professor Phillips. Welcome. Would you like some water, coffee, or something to drink?"

"*No, grazie.*"

"Come this way," she said as she accompanied him down the hallway to a large conference room.

Mr. Alberti and Mr. Caruso sat across from two other men and a forty-year-old woman, well dressed.

Alberti stood and made introductions. "Julian, this is Bianca, Piero's niece. And these are her lawyers, Mr. Russo and Mr. Salvatori."

"*Piacere*," they all said in unison, shaking hands across the table.

Bianca wore a stiff black business dress, high heels, and a turquoise scarf. She and Julian had met years ago at a family reunion. Bianca smiled warmly, eager to take possession of the residence she always felt should have been her father's and not Marcella's.

Mr. Alberti invited everyone to take a seat and then opened a folder. He cleared his throat and began, "We seem to have a little problem."

Bianca shifted anxiously in her chair, and her lawyers looked nervously at her and then at Mr. Alberti.

"It seems that Marcella amended the trust."

"I thought the trust was irrevocable," Mr. Russo interjected. "What kind of amendments would be possible?"

"As you know, per the trust, the residence must stay within the family. Marcella inherited it. Her husband is the surviving beneficiary." Mr. Alberti looked over at Julian, who nodded.

Mr. Salvatori then interjected, "And if Professor Phillips wants to sell, he can and must offer it to the first of Piero's nieces and nephews – in this case, Bianca."

"That's where we have a little problem. Marcella added a provision that when her daughters came of age, they would have the right of first refusal if their father decided to sell the property."

"How old are they?" Mr. Russo inquired, looking at Julian.

"Twenty-one and nineteen," Julian replied.

"The twenty-one-year-old has the right of first refusal. Before we can transfer title to the property, she would have to give permission," Mr. Caruso noted.

"Why didn't you bring this up earlier," Mr. Salvatori inquired.

"It seems that the addendum was added just a short while ago, when Marcella was ill. I was out of town and didn't notice it until I was reviewing the documents for today," Mr. Alberti said. Then he continued, "Julian, can I confer with you privately?"

He nodded. They left the conference room and went into Alberti's office.

"Wow," Julian said. "This is a major development and problem."

Alberti nodded. "I'm sorry we didn't catch this earlier. What would you like to do?"

"I need to talk to Luna."

Alberti nodded. "Do you want to call her? I'm sure we could document a conversation if she agrees to release the option."

"No. I think this demands an in-person conversation with her. I'll see if she can fly over this week."

"As you wish," Alberti said, secretly delighted that there would be a delay in the transaction.

"Is there anything more we need to do today? Any information you need from me?"

"No. Just let me know once you've spoken with your daughter and she decides."

Julian stood, shook Alberti's hand, and left the offices and building. He wandered across the Tiber into the medieval historical center of Rome, perplexed by Marcella's secret move. He called his daughter.

"Hey dad, what's up?" she said as she answered the phone.

"Hey, love. How's it going with you?"

"I'm fine. Missing you."

"I miss you, too. *Senti*, we have to talk."

"What's the matter?"

"As you know, I was going to sell the apartment. Today, we discovered that your mom stipulated that you would have the right of first refusal if I offered it for sale."

"What does that mean?" Luna inquired.

"I can't sell it unless you decide you don't want it."

"What am I going to do with an antique apartment in Rome? How would I buy it?"

"Well, if you wanted to buy it and keep it, I would give you some of her trust. Or, if you and Livia want to keep it, I will keep it for the three of us."

"I thought you wanted to get rid of the responsibilities associated with maintaining it."

"I do. And it's too painful to be here in the house."

"Why do you think mom inserted that stipulation?"

"Well, you know her. She had such a strong attachment to the house. I don't think she wanted to see it go to a cousin. Why don't you come over and we can talk?"

"Sure. Let me see if I can get a flight this evening. I could be there tomorrow," she said, sensing her dad was agitated and unsettled. "Are you okay?"

"Yeah, dear. It's just been a stressful couple of weeks. It would be nice to have you here."

The next day, Julian stood outside the customs area of Leonardo Da Vinci airport waiting for his daughter. The scent of the salt air from the nearby beach at Ostia troubled him, a vexing reminder of Bruno. Bruno had texted multiple times, asking how things went and whether they might talk before he left for Berlin and eventually for the States. Julian hadn't responded to the texts.

Luna exited through the opaque doors and searched for her dad. When he caught her eyes, he felt his knees weaken. She looked so much like Marcella, with her brunette hair, blond highlights, and caramel skin.

"Oh Luna, it's so good to see you," he said as he gave her a warm hug and kiss.

"It's good to see you. I didn't think I'd be back here so soon."

"Well, let's make the best of it."

Luna gazed at her father and saw weariness in his eyes. "What's the matter?"

"It's a long story, some of which probably isn't worth sharing," he began. "Let's get a taxi and head into town."

They quickly found a taxi and sped into the center of Rome. Luna hadn't been to the city in over two years, the last ones spent tending to her mom's illness and commuting between Atlanta and New York for school. They pulled up to the apartment, paid the driver, and walked up the stairs into the home.

Luna was quiet and solemn, honoring the memory of her mother and grandparents as she entered the space. Julian gave her a warm hug, took her bags into the guestroom, and invited her to take a seat in the parlor. "Would you like some coffee, something to eat, something to drink?"

"I'm not hungry, but I wouldn't mind a glass of wine."

"*Subito*," he said, retreating to the kitchen and returning with a cold bottle of white and two glasses.

"How are you doing?" Luna began.

"I should ask you that question. I can't imagine losing a mom at your age."

"I'm okay, dad. But you don't seem like you are."

Julian looked off into the distance and then turned to her.

"I'm okay. I'm just sad."

Luna nodded. "So, what's this about the trust?"

"Did your mom ever say anything about the house to you?"

Luna looked away evasively. "Luna?" Julian pressed.

"Well, she and I had a conversation not too long before she passed."

Julian inched toward the edge of his seat and took a big sip of wine.

"She said something about having made sacrifices ‑ something about all of us making sacrifices in life for the sake of traditions, for the sake of heritage."

"She came from a long line of noble Roman families, and her father, your grandfather, was certainly a formidable dynastic figure," Julian noted.

Luna smiled and then said, "She also said something strange. It made little sense to me. She said, 'When I pass, your father will have a tough time. I know him. He's going to want to cut cords, make a clean break. He will face a crisis of identity, and I need you to help him through it.'"

Julian shook his head.

"I don't think she wanted you to walk away from your Roman connections. It is too much a part of who you are. Maybe that's why she was making it more difficult to sell the apartment."

Julian nodded. "Yes, I can see her orchestrating that," he said. Deep down, he wondered if Marcella knew there were other crises he would face at her death, the questioning of his affections and the turbulence he would face untethered from her.

"Are you okay, dad? You seem different."

"Yes. I'm fine. It will take some time to heal. I'm looking forward to returning to Atlanta and spending time with you and Livia. So," he continued, wringing his hands, "what do you think about selling the place?"

"It's not my decision. It's really yours."

"But obviously, mom wanted you to be part of the decision."

"I like it here, but I've never felt like Rome was home. It was a great place to visit and a fantasy to be bi-national and fly back and forth in the summers and holidays. But home is Atlanta – or perhaps New York, now."

"Why don't we spend some time here and decide later. There's no hurry, and you're on summer break, right? We could go to the beach, travel, see some exhibits – whatever you'd like."

Luna nodded warmly. "That would be nice."

"Let's get you unpacked. I'm sure you would like to clean up and you must have jet lag."

They walked back to the guestroom and unpacked. Luna took a shower and then laid down on the bed, falling into a deep jetlag induced sleep.

17

Chapter Seventeen – Bruno

The next day, Luna rose early and made herself an espresso in the kitchen. Julian was already working on the codex in Piero's study. She walked to the window and looked out over the excavations of Trajan's forum and the busy Piazza Venezia. She glanced down and noticed an artist had set up his easel on the far edge of the excavations and was prepping his canvas and materials.

He was handsome. He had dark, thick hair, a closely trimmed beard, and muscular arms, shoulders, and legs. He stood back from the canvas he had secured and looked up at the window. Luna recoiled slightly, but was intrigued and continued to watch him. She was puzzled by the fact that he was not focusing on Trajan's column or on the cupola of Santissimo Nome di Maria, but on the apartment building itself.

The artist paused as he caught Luna's gaze. He looked surprised and bewildered. He shook his head, squinted his eyes, and stretched his neck beyond the canvas toward her. She got anxious and stepped away from the window and walked into her grandfather's study.

"Dad, there's an artist outside who looks like he's painting our building."

Julian blushed, closed his laptop, stood, and walked toward the window, peering around the corner of the window frame inconspicuously.

"Do you know him?" she asked, noting his reticence to stand fully in the window.

Julian didn't respond.

"Dad? What's up?"

"I don't know, dear. It's odd, isn't it? I've never seen an artist take that perspective before. Maybe he's using our building as the background for his composition. Yes. I'm sure that must be the case."

Julian walked back into the study. Luna made another espresso and returned to the window. The artist was sitting on a bench with his chin resting on the back of his hands, deep in thought.

Bruno was taken aback at seeing Luna in the window. She was the splitting image of Marcella, the younger Marcella, the Marcella he had been in love with. After thirty years, his heart still pounded and his pulse raced as he observed her smile, her hair, her beautiful, luminous skin. Just yesterday, Julian had taken off to sign papers and fly to Berlin. This couldn't be his niece. It had to be Marcella's daughter, Julian's daughter. But it didn't make sense.

Julian heard the door open and Luna head down the marble steps. He glanced out the window and saw her circle the archaeological park and approach Bruno.

"*Ciao*," she said to him.

"*Ciao*," Bruno replied.

"I saw you setting up to paint and wondered if you were going to paint our building."

"Yes. Do you mind?"

"No. It would be a nice memento. My father is selling it, and it would be nice to have something tangible I could bring home. I would love to buy whatever you paint."

Bruno couldn't take his eyes off Luna and kept murmuring to himself, "Amazing. The resemblance is uncanny."

"*Ma chi è Lei?*" Bruno inquired of her identity, introducing himself, "*Mi chiamo Bruno.*"

"Luna Phillips. *Piacere.* My father owns the building there, but he wants to sell it. My mother just passed."

Bruno wanted to say, 'I know. I know your father and your mother.' But he checked his impulse and asked instead, "Ah. Interesting. How soon are you moving?"

"We're not sure. There are some matters we need to sort out. How quickly could you finish a painting?"

"Well, that all depends," Bruno began, wondering how he might delay things.

"Here's my card. Can you let me know when you have something finished for me to look at?"

Bruno nodded, took the card, and placed it in the front pocket of his shirt.

"*Grazie,*" she said, extending her hand. Bruno delayed retracting his hand, attempting to extract any trace of Marcella from their exchange. Luna looked at him curiously and returned to the apartment.

At the top of the stairs, Julian was waiting. "Who was that?"

"An artist. I wanted to see if he was going to paint our building. It would be a nice memorial we could take back with us."

Julian placed his arm around Luna's shoulder and walked her back into the parlor. He was nervous Bruno might knock on the door. "Should we go out today and have lunch, take a stroll through the city?"

"I would like that. It's been a while."

"Let's get dressed."

Julian walked down the hall to his and Marcella's room, pulled the drapes closed, and looked through a slit in the material at Bruno. His heart pounded as he watched him make initial brush strokes on the canvas. He walked toward the armoire to retrieve some jeans and a shirt when he felt his phone vibrate. It was a text from Bruno: "Are you still in Rome? Let's talk."

He didn't respond. He dressed and met Luna in the parlor. "Shall we?" he asked as he slipped his sunglasses on.

Luna nodded as she looked around the space.

As they left the building, Julian held his daughter tightly and pivoted in the opposite direction of where Bruno was painting, hastening toward the historical center of Rome.

"It's good to be with you," he said. "Maybe it was fortuitous that mom put a provision in the trust. It forced us to take this time together in Rome."

"Mom always had a way of making things like that happen. It's funny, since her passing, it's been hard to remember her. I feel like she's slipping away – her smile, her smell, her laugh. When I walked into the apartment yesterday, it was as if she were there, physically. I could sense her and feel her. It was strange. I dreamed of her last night, the first since she passed."

Julian nodded, remembering his own recent dream of her.

They walked into the Piazza Rotonda. People were scurrying back and forth on their way to work, and tourists were lining up to enter the Pantheon. "Didn't you and mom get married there?" she asked.

Julian, choked with emotion, nodded.

They continued past the square and onto a small lane lined with boutique shops. Luna held her dad tightly as she peered into the windows and imagined her mom going inside and chatting with the clerks. She had been effervescent and full of life. Everyone knew her and looked forward to her visits. Luna and Julian continued their walk through the shopping district, past the Spanish Steps, past the Trevi Fountain, and finally to Julian's favorite trattoria, where Angelo greeted them warmly.

They sat and ordered wine and salads. "What's up," Julian inquired of Luna who seemed lost in thought.

"It's funny. When you mentioned selling the place, it made sense to me. Mom isn't here. She was our connection to Rome. With her gone, the city seemed to have lost its appeal."

Julian nodded. "Yes, that was my experience as well."

"But since I arrived, it has differed from what I imagined. It's as if she's present. I can feel her holding my hand and laughing. I can smell her and feel her warmth. Maybe we should keep the place and spend more time here. I don't want to forget her."

Julian creased his forehead.

"Sorry, dad," Luna added. "Maybe it's too painful for you."

"I don't want to deprive you of a connection you can have with your mother. She would have loved it if you and Livia wanted to spend more time here, make Rome your home."

"While she was alive, I enjoyed coming to Rome, but it never felt like home. I couldn't wait to get back to my friends, to school, to Atlanta."

Julian smiled.

Angelo came to the table and took orders for their main course. Luna ordered a seafood risotto and Julian veal scallopini. Julian took a sip of wine and breathed in the air. He glanced around the terrace at the other tables and nodded as several business executives caught his eye. He recognized them as Piero's associates.

"So, if we kept the place, what would we do with it? It seems a shame to have this enormous space empty most of the time. Could we rent it out?" Luna inquired.

"I know. That's my dilemma. What sense does it make to keep it?"

"What about renting it out?"

"I'm not sure the bylaws of the association would allow that and, besides, I'm not sure I want people coming in and out of the place. It's too valuable for that."

"What about your work? Could you do more projects here? Aren't you doing one now?"

"I could. But I'm not sure that's what I want to do. Atlanta's home. Rome is a nice place to visit from time to time," Julian said unconvincingly.

Luna put her hand on her father's and said, "And what about your future? I'm sure mom would want you to date and be happy. That's not likely to happen here."

Julian's heart skipped a beat, and he blushed.

"Dad?" Luna said, out of concern for his change of pallor.

"It's nothing. Just the heat."

They continued lunch and returned to the residence. Bruno had already packed and headed home. Luna took a nap, and Julian checked emails and messages. Bruno had texted several times, pleading for them to talk.

The next day, Luna got a call from Bruno. "Luna, this is Bruno, the artist from yesterday. I have something I would like to show you. Would you and your dad like to come to my studio?"

"Let me check. I'll call you back. Is this a good number?"

"Sure. *A presto.*"

"Dad, the artist would like to show us a painting. Are you up for a visit to his studio?"

"No. Why don't you go. I have work to do," he said.

"Okay. You don't mind?"

Julian searched for a reason to dissuade her, but couldn't come up with anything. "Sure. Why don't you see what he has to show you?" he suggested, his hand trembling.

An hour later, Luna knocked on Bruno's door. He unlatched the lock and asked her to enter. "Welcome. I'm glad you could come."

"My pleasure. What a nice place."

"Yes. I inherited it from my parents. My studio is on the top floor. Shall we?"

They walked up the stairs. The light flooded the stairwell, and Luna gasped as she walked into the studio space and saw his work. "Wow! This is amazing."

Bruno grinned in delight. He walked her around the room and showed her things he was working on.

"Your work is familiar. I think I've seen some of your pieces before. Maybe my grandfather has some. The use of light and the focus on ancient structures is something he would have gravitated to."

"Hmm," Bruno murmured, intrigued by another coincidence. "And here's the piece I'm working on of your home."

"Oh my God," she began. "You did this the other day?"

Bruno nodded. "I still have some things to adjust and fix, but the basic composition is there."

"It's magnificent. I'm not sure I ever appreciated what our place looks like, particularly with the excavations in the foreground. It's phenomenal. I would have thought you would have focused on the columns, but instead, the building is the focus, and the excavations are an impressionistic play of light and color. It's beautiful."

"You should be very proud of the place. I'm surprised your father wants to sell it."

"Well, my mom passed. I think it's painful for him."

"I can imagine. So, you like the painting?"

Luna nodded.

"It's yours."

"No. I want to buy it from you," Luna said, her eyes wide in surprise.

"It's a gift. I've admired your building for years, and your grandfather was such a promoter of Roman heritage and art. It's a fitting tribute to him."

"You know my grandfather?"

Bruno realized he had slipped and said too much. "I knew of him. Everyone did."

Luna sighed.

"Would you like something to drink downstairs?"

Luna nodded. "Can I use the bathroom first?"

"Sure." He walked her down to the second floor and said, "The bath is there, on the right."

Luna walked into the tiled antique room and closed the door. As she sat on the toilette, she looked up at the door in front of her. Hanging on a hook was a polo shirt, one that she recognized for its distinctive color and brand. The color had faded, a peach-pink blend that Marcella always said looked good on her father, showcasing his tan skin and dark hair. A boutique in Atlanta was the exclusive vendor of the shirt. She gasped. She finished peeing and walked down the hall and downstairs into the parlor.

She scrutinized Bruno as he prepared a platter of cheese and opened a bottle of wine. "So, why our residence? Why were you painting it?"

Bruno was caught off-guard. "By chance. I specialize in archaeological paintings. I have done several renditions of Trajan's Forum, but never from the angle looking toward your building. I wanted to experiment."

"You mentioned my grandfather. You didn't, by chance, know my mother, Marcella?"

Bruno could hardly contain himself. Hearing her name and looking at Luna was unsettling. Luna noticed his hesitation and pressed him further, "Come to think of it, my mother mentioned an artist she knew in Rome. She spoke fondly of him. I can't remember his name."

Marcella had never mentioned him to Luna, but Luna was a master at extracting information, and she believed Bruno might be forthcoming with the right bait.

"Maybe I met her at a show or exposition. Who knows?"

"It would be an interesting coincidence, no?" Luna asked.

"Yes, indeed."

They continued to chat about Rome, about art, and about Luna's studies. Eventually, Luna said, "Well. I don't want to take more of your time. Can I buy the painting from you?"

"It still needs a little work. Can you come back later in the week?"

"Sure. Let me know when and how much, and I'll come back. By the way, can I use the bathroom one more time?"

"Sure. I think you know the way."

Luna returned to the bathroom, took the shirt off the hook, giving it a quick sniff to see if she detected her dad's scent. It smelled of salt and sunscreen. She rolled it tightly and placed it in her bag and headed back downstairs.

"Thank you so much," she said, extending her hand to Bruno. Bruno leaned into her and gave her a kiss on both cheeks.

"*Piacere*."

"*Ciao*."

Back at the apartment, Luna approached her dad in the study.

"So, how was the painting?"

"It's incredible. He works quickly."

"Hmm," Julian murmured.

"Dad, let's talk."

Julian looked alarmed, wondering if Bruno had said anything to her. In fact, the whole time she was away, he fretted over possible disclosures.

"Sure, dear. Would you like some coffee?"

"That would be nice."

They walked into the kitchen, and Julian prepared a couple of espressos.

Luna opened her bag and extracted the shirt. She laid it on the counter, saying nothing. Julian looked at her, and she at him.

"Ah," Julian finally said. "You must have found that."

"Yes," she said. "Who is Bruno?"

18

Chapter Eighteen – Mourning

Bruno sat across from Julian at the little wine bar near Bruno's studio. Neither knew how or where to start. They sipped their wine and played nervously with their napkins. Finally, Bruno said, "There's more you should know."

Julian looked alarmed.

"I always thought Marcella was having an affair and, when I discovered your connection, I concluded you had stolen her away from me. The other day, I had a long talk with Marianna and Gabriella, and Gabriella filled me in. Marcella had every intention of marrying me, but her father opposed the marriage. He said I was too common, and that I had no future as an artist."

"That's horrible, but not surprising coming from Piero."

Bruno nodded. "Gabriella said Marcella was going to go through with the marriage until her father threatened to cut her off from the estate. She ultimately gave into her father."

"Ah, well, that's probably why she made some comment to Luna about making sacrifices for tradition and for the family."

Bruno nodded. He hung his head low. "I'm sorry I got angry at you."

Julian looked disoriented. He took a long sip of wine and glanced away from the table. Bruno noticed a tear running down Julian's cheek and said, "Julian, what's the matter?"

More tears flowed, and Julian sobbed, hiding his face in the folds of his napkin. Bruno placed his hand on Julian's. A few minutes later, Julian wiped his eyes dry and said, "That's the first time I've cried since she passed."

"I'm sure it has been difficult losing her," Bruno said thoughtfully.

"I think this is worse," Julian remarked.

Bruno creased his forehead, seeking clarification.

"All of our married life I struggled to be the husband I thought Marcella wanted, the husband Marcella deserved. Part of the pressure was living up to Piero's and Camilla's expectations, but I also wanted Marcella to be happy, and I never sensed she was. Now I know why. I was her back-up plan, the classics professor who would appease her father and be the support she needed."

Bruno had difficulty thinking Marcella hadn't found Julian attractive and sexy, although he could see Julian being the typical nerdy professor, and that wasn't Marcella's type. He realized Julian was perhaps mourning not so much Marcella's death but the death of their marriage, the death of the idea he had of their marriage.

"And your daughter? Luna? How's she?"

"Surprised but remarkably supportive."

Bruno sighed in relief. "She's the splitting image of Marcella, the younger Marcella."

"I know. When I saw her at the airport the other day, it hit me how much she resembles her."

"So, she's not upset with you?"

"She has so many gay friends in New York that it doesn't faze her. She thinks it's cool, intriguing – like I finally came out of my shell. She wants to meet you."

"We already did."

"She wants to meet you and me together."

"Does that mean there's a chance for a me and you together?"

Julian shook his head, still nursing the raw emotions of the past several days. "I don't know what I was thinking. I lost my head."

"No, you embraced a side of yourself that was always there just below the surface."

"I don't know if I can do this. And, frankly, I'm not sure you can."

"Give us a chance. You might be surprised. Why don't we have dinner with Luna?"

Julian hesitated and took a long sip of his wine. He gazed off into the distance and then turned to Bruno. "I guess that wouldn't be so onerous."

Bruno smiled. "Tomorrow night? Our usual?"

Julian nodded. They finished their wine, embraced, and returned to their respective homes.

The next evening, Julian stood in front of the mirror in his bathroom and washed his face, brushed his hair, and buttoned a loose cotton summer shirt. He had on a pair of tight-fitting jeans and casual leather sneakers. Luna approached the doorway and said, "You're so handsome. It was only a matter of time before the gays would go after you."

Julian looked at his daughter, his eyes filled with questions.

"You know mom had a lot of gay friends in Atlanta," Luna noted.

"I didn't know that. I guess I was naïve. I thought they were part of her art crowd, philanthropists, cultural leaders."

"Who do you think most of those people are?"

"Hmm," he murmured, realizing that perhaps he had been oblivious where he should have been more observant. "Shall we go? If we don't leave soon, I'll lose my nerve and back out."

"*Andiamo*," she said, grabbing her father's arm and heading down the hall and toward the stairway. Once outside, they made their way across the Piazza Venezia and into the maze of narrow roads and lanes surrounding Campo de' Fiori and the Via Giulia.

"It's this way," Julian said, guiding his daughter toward the brightly lit outdoor terrace of the neighborhood trattoria. Bruno was standing on the street, checking messages on his phone. He looked up and gasped for air as he saw Julian and Luna approach.

Bruno embraced and kissed Luna and then embraced Julian, giving him a protracted, affectionate kiss on his cheek.

A server showed them a table. Bruno sat across from Luna, and Julian sat on the other end of the table between them. Bruno ordered wine and antipasti as Julian and Luna observed in silence.

"Well," Bruno began, "I'm glad we could do this."

Luna nodded and smiled. There was an awkward silence, no one knowing exactly where to start. Luna put her hand on top of her father's and said, "Tell me again how you guys met. It's still unbelievable."

Julian began recounting their bumping into each other at archaeological sites. He described his first visit to Bruno's studio and their excursion to Ostia.

"Wasn't that where you and mom met?" Luna asked.

Bruno looked at Julian inquisitively. Julian cleared his throat nervously and said, "Yes, that's where we first met."

Julian recounted his meeting Marcella, and Bruno became visibly more restless. He glanced over at Luna and felt calmer. Julian continued to recount his and Bruno's adventures, but Bruno paid no attention, instead traveling in his mind to his own youth. Luna looked over and caught Bruno's eyes. Bruno didn't look away. He gazed into her deeply set hazel eyes and soaked in her radiance, her luminous skin, her affable smile, and her warmth.

Self-consciously, Luna looked down and fidgeted with her napkin, glancing over at her father, deep in the details of his story. Bruno realized he had made her uncomfortable and turned his attention to Julian, who seemed oblivious to the fact that his audience had been elsewhere.

When Julian finished, Bruno looked up at Luna and said, "Tell me about you. What was it like growing up in Atlanta and Rome? What a fascinating childhood you must have had."

Luna had the same mannerisms as her mother. She turned toward Bruno, but her body faced Julian. She placed her right hand at the center of her chest and grabbed a pendant hanging from her neck, and played with it as she spoke. She peppered her discourse with Italian phrases and used her eyes to emphasize points here and there. She had a silky voice and sensuous lips, and Bruno felt himself falling under her spell.

"And boyfriends in Atlanta or New York?" he inquired.

Luna blushed and looked nervously at her father. Julian said, "Go on, I'm not listening."

"No one in particular. I have a nice circle of friends. We hang out a lot. The scene in New York is great – and it's not bad in Atlanta, either."

"Friends here?" Bruno pressed.

"Curiously, no. When we were here, it was always with family."

"But you must have turned heads here," he said and then looked at Julian and added, "Sorry, maybe that's not what a father wants to hear."

"No, she's a charming young lady, and yes, she's a head turner."

"Dad!"

Bruno became more animated. He leaned toward Luna as they spoke. Julian noticed and became alarmed.

They ordered, ate, visited, and then glanced at watches as they downed espressos. Bruno said, "Do you want to go out to a club?"

Julian and Luna looked at each other, lifted their shoulders as if to say, 'well, what do you think?' and in unison said, "Sure. Do you have a place in mind?"

Bruno nodded, grabbed Luna's hand, and led them off across the river into Trastevere. They walked farther and approached an unremarkable building with a short line of people at the door waiting to get in. "This is a great place," Bruno said.

"Do you come here often?" Julian inquired.

"I wouldn't say often. But when I have friends in town, this is where we go to dance and have a drink."

Soon they were let in. The owners had converted the building into a cavernous bar with an expansive area for dancing. Loud music echoed against the walls, and colorful disco lights sparkled. Bruno ordered drinks, and they stood at the edge of the dance area enjoying the music. Bruno set his drink down on a high-top table and asked Luna and Julian to dance. The three of them inched into the crowd and moved to the music.

Bruno smiled effusively. He glanced around the room as he danced, but continued to circle back to Luna. She was beautiful and had a graceful body. She was an excellent dancer, unlike her father, who did little more than rock back and forth. Julian observed his daughter and Bruno and became increasingly alarmed at the energy growing between them. She seemed to love the attention of the hot Italian guy in front of her, and Bruno seemed lost in her radiance.

Julian signaled he was going to take a break, and Bruno and Luna remained dancing. Julian quickly finished his drink and ordered a second. "*Cazzo*," he said to himself, realizing that not only might Bruno not be gay, but he was falling for his daughter. What kind of twisted fate were the Roman gods dishing out that promised to make his nightmare even worse.

Bruno and Luna took a break, and the three of them continued to nurse their drinks and look out into the crowd. To Julian's relief, a couple of younger men approached Luna and chatted. They offered her another drink, and one of them invited her to dance. She handed her drink to Julian, who watched as she receded into the crowd.

Awkwardly, Julian stood next to Bruno. Bruno said, "Your daughter is so beautiful and full of life. You must be proud of her."

Julian wasn't amused. But just as he was about to make some snarky comment to Bruno, Bruno added, "But it is her father who is the hottie here."

"What?" Julian asked.

"You heard me. I'm standing next to the real hottie of the room."

Julian felt himself become aroused. Bruno looked evasively across the dancefloor but continued to lob affectionate bombs at Julian. "You know, if Luna gets lucky, her father might get luckier."

Bruno then turned and gazed into Julian's eyes. "We have to talk."

"Now?"

"The sooner the better."

Julian rehearsed several options in his head and settled on one. When his daughter finished dancing and joined them, he said, "Dear, I think we've had enough. Do you want to stay? We'll head home."

"No. I'm good to go, too. Great place!" she added, looking at Bruno.

"Would you mind if Bruno came to our place for an after-party drink?"

"Not at all. I'd like that."

Julian looked at Bruno, who, even without an explicit invitation, nodded yes.

They left the club and took a taxi to Piazza Venezia. Julian led the two of them up the marble staircase into the grand residence. As

Julian turned on a few lights, Bruno's eyes widened, and his mouth opened in astonishment.

"Wow! What a space!" he said.

"You've never been here? Even with mom?" Luna inquired.

"No. When I knew your mom, her grandparents lived here. They never invited me. This is my first visit."

Julian took him for a tour and stopped in the dining room to show him the two paintings Piero had of his. "Ah, yes, these were two that had won prizes at a competition. I think Marcella must have given them to Piero to convince him of my future. It obviously didn't work."

Luna went into the kitchen and drank a large glass of water. She came back out into the dining area and sensed her dad wanted to be alone with Bruno and said, "Thanks for a great evening. I think I need to get some sleep. Jet lag's still hanging on a bit."

Julian kissed his daughter good night.

"Luna, it was so nice to meet you at last. What a beautiful person you are!" Bruno embraced her warmly.

"The pleasure was all mine."

As she walked down the hall, Julian asked Bruno, "Can I get you a brandy or something?"

"That would be nice. We need to talk."

Julian poured them each a generous brandy, and they sat side by side on one of the sofas.

Bruno began nervously, "Your daughter is amazing. She's so beautiful and charming and sophisticated. She's got a great personality – affable like her mom and thoughtful like her dad."

Julian blushed.

"I have to admit that I was smitten. She is vexing. She is so much like Marcella, and I found myself transported back in time."

"I was afraid of that."

"But as the evening progressed, I had gnawing feelings of inadequacy."

"Well, she's slightly younger than you," Julian noted. "It would take a lot for her to make the leap to a middle-aged man, even as handsome as you."

"Be nice!"

Bruno reached over and took Julian's hand and rubbed it. "As we were dancing, a thought came over me. I kept looking over at you."

"If you did, you could have fooled me. You seemed glued to her."

"You didn't notice?"

"Regretfully, no."

"I kept looking at you. Suddenly, I had an epiphany, a strange flash-back. I remember dancing with Marcella. She was so beautiful, affable, and sexy. She was the life of the party, and I couldn't believe I was with her. But the recollection I had tonight was different. I remember now being intrigued by the sexy guys dancing near us and by the languorous poses of men leaning against the bar, their shirts unbuttoned and their muscular frames all-too-apparent. Marcella was unattainable, but not because she didn't love me, but because I was attracted to men. I couldn't admit it then. My father would have killed me. I'm sure I idealized our relationship and used it as an excuse to avoid accepting my orientation. All of that changed with you. I don't know what it was or is about you, but it became undeniable. I love men. I love you."

Bruno was dumbfounded and speechless.

"It was seeing your daughter and facing the memory of Marcella that finally broke the spell."

"Wow," Julian said. "I didn't expect that."

"Me, neither," Bruno said, his eyes fixed on Julian's.

Julian stood and took Bruno's hand. He began leading him down the hallway to the master bedroom. He turned on a few small table lamps and closed the drapes. A soft glow filled the room. Julian stood facing Bruno and began to unbutton his shirt.

"Professor?" Bruno feigned shock.

"Shh," he said, holding his finger up to Bruno's mouth. He then traced it over Bruno's lips and leaned toward him, giving him a deep, warm kiss.

Bruno grabbed Julian around his torso, lifted him a few inches, and carried him toward the bed, pushing him down on the soft mattress. He bent over, unbuckled Julian's belt and unzipped his jeans, feeling the hardness pressing against his undershorts. He pulled Julian's jeans down off his legs and ran his hands up his thighs. "I've always loved runner's legs."

"You mean there are others?"

"I've only looked." Then Bruno held his finger up to Julian's lips and said, "Shh."

Bruno ripped the front of his shirt open, a couple of buttons popping loose. He reached down and unzipped his pants and dropped them on the floor. He then reclined on Julian, sliding his hand up under Julian's polo shirt and caressing his smooth pecs. "You're so hot!"

Julian kissed Bruno. They explored the warm moistness between them, and they both felt their pulse race as their hard shafts throbbed in anticipation. Bruno reached down and slid his hand up through the leg of Julian's undershorts, taking hold of his hardness and stroking it tenderly. The sensation of Bruno penetrating the tight fabric was arousing, and he felt himself lose control.

He slid his shorts off and felt the heat of Bruno's flesh pressed against him. He reached behind Bruno and squeezed his firm buttocks while Bruno licked Julian's ear and the nape of his neck.

They both abandoned themselves to the frenzy of their passion, neither wanting to hurry their climax. They savored each other's bodies, the texture of each other's skin, the earthy and masculine smell each emanated, and the tenderness and longing filling their eyes.

Bruno felt years of shame and regret lifting from his chest, finally giving his heart to Julian, whose arms made him feel secure and loved. Julian, for the first time, felt in synch with his body and confident in his ability to love. After coming, they collapsed in the folds of each other's embrace, and fell into a peaceful sleep. At one point, Julian rose to pee. He glanced around the room. A few errant beams of light from streetlamps reflected off the walls and ceiling. He always felt that Piero's room would make him feel creepy, that he would feel like an interloper in an alien land. He took a deep breath and realized he was home, that he could make this his home.

19

Chapter Nineteen – A Year Later

"Julian, what a fabulous reception," Luciana said as she approached him with a glass of wine and gave her colleague kisses on his cheeks.

A group of colleagues, friends, and admirers encircled Julian. Luca was holding Julian's hand playfully as Julian described the reaction of one of the ministers of culture to a new exhibit of homoerotic art in Gabriella's gallery.

"You could tell he was turned on, but he kept gesticulating disdain in a high-pitched voice," Julian said as his audience laughed.

"*Vuoi un po' di vino?*" Luca asked Julian as he noticed his glass was empty.

Julian nodded.

Luca went to the wine bar and refilled their glasses. He bumped into Stefano and Giorgio, who were admiring the art on the walls.

"Luca, isn't that one of Bruno's?" they asked, pointing to a painting near the dining area.

He nodded as he indicated he was on a mission. He returned to Julian, who took the drink and toasted his friends.

Sofia approached Luciana and kissed Julian. "Julian, *auguri!*"

"Thanks. I'm glad you're here to celebrate. You must be proud of Luciana."

"I am. But this is about you and your work. The translation and notes are marvelous and have set off a whole fresh interest in late Roman studies."

"Luciana had the vision."

"And you the expertise and sensitivity to tone and nuance."

Julian spotted his two daughters, Luna and Livia, across the room chatting with Gabriella. She had taken them shopping for clothes, and they were certainly being noticed by several handsome young men. He was proud of them. They had insisted throughout their lives that Marcella speak to them in Italian, and it paid off. They were fluent and quite enchanting.

Mr. Alberti and Mr. Caruso approached Julian. "*Auguri!* What a glorious celebration!"

"I'm glad you made it, and I'm glad you and Luna talked me out of selling this to Bianca. This is what Marcella would have wanted."

"We agree. She loved Rome, and she loved her home. It was too bad she and Piero seemed so tense with each other later in life."

"I was always baffled by that, but I've come to appreciate the roots of it. I'm just glad we've kept the place in the family."

They nodded. "And we like what you've done with it," Mr. Caruso noted. "You've kept the architectural bones and layout, but the furnishings are more contemporary."

"I hope it's not too modern," Julian said, looking at some of those gathered around him.

Gino, one of the editors of the codex translation and commentary, said, "Not at all. This is an outstanding example of how to blend classical elements with modern pieces. I have a feeling you may be approached by some editors who want to feature the place in a magazine."

Julian nodded excitedly.

Mr. Caruso inquired, "So, I hear you're not going back to Atlanta?"

"That's right. Luciana was able to secure some grants for work at the Capitoline Museums, and I have a couple of courses lined up at the Sapienza. I sold my home in Atlanta. With Marcella's estate, I can maintain this residence and work here."

"We couldn't be more excited," Mr. Caruso remarked. "We weren't crazy about Piero's niece. She would never have appreciated this place as you do."

"It took some getting used to. I was always intimidated by it. It never felt like home. I've made peace with the house. We're friends, now," he said, winking.

Caruso looked at him curiously, as if he had spoken some strange new language.

Julian looked up from Caruso and noticed Bruno coming into the parlor. He wore a tailored, tight-fitting dark blue suit that showcased his physique. The white linen dress shirt showed off his summer tan. His deep set, dark alluring eyes beckoned from across the expansive space. Julian's heart began to pound, and his pulse raced as Bruno approached.

Journalists pressed toward him, and photographers snapped photos for the articles that would appear in the morning papers. He beamed with delight at the attention.

He caught Julian's eyes, and they gazed at each other. Julian nodded and smiled. Bruno acknowledged him briefly before he was pulled off to the side for an interview.

Eventually, he extracted himself from the reporters and walked toward Julian. He leaned toward him, gave him a kiss, and they stood side-by-side as Gabriella approached the podium and taped the microphone.

"Ladies and gentlemen. *Benvenuti!* What a momentous occasion. First, I want to congratulate Luciana Alfano and her team for the work they did, creating a wonderful exhibit. It was only a year ago that Luciana asked Julian to translate and write a commentary on the Ostia codex. In record time, he produced a tight but nuanced translation and was able to provide invaluable analysis as to its significance in helping us understand late Roman life and the transition from traditional Roman religion to Christianity. His work has inspired a new generation of scholars."

Everyone applauded. Julian nodded and beamed.

"We're also here to celebrate a new exhibition of Bruno Muzzi. Muzzi is unparalleled in his renditions of classic Roman sites. His work brings to life the subtle light and texture of ancient Rome. Some of the pieces of the show are here on display," she said as she pointed to several easels set up in the space. "As you know, there will be a live auction later of an unusual piece he did of Capri. The proceeds will go to the Capitoline Museums to support the Ostia Codex project."

Everyone applauded. Bruno turned toward Julian and beamed. Julian took Bruno's hand and squeezed it warmly.

Gabriella finished her speech, inviting people to the gallery and encouraging them to enjoy the reception, food, and drink. She approached Julian and Bruno, gave them both kisses, and said, "Congratulations. What a great event."

"It wouldn't have been the same without your vision and contacts," Julian said.

"You've been such an inspiration to Bruno. His work has become more luminous," Gabriella remarked.

"I can't believe that. They were already filled with light."

"I know. But there's something different about them. They have a serenity to them that certainly rises from his newfound peace. Are you guys going to take a break after these events?"

Julian nodded. "I think so. We haven't decided yet, but we would like to take some time and travel."

Marianna walked up, gave Gabriella, Julian, and Bruno kisses on her cheeks. "*Auguri* to you both."

"*Grazie*. Thanks for being here."

"Are you kidding? I wouldn't miss this event for all the money in the world. You know you guys are the new talk of the town."

Bruno and Julian looked inquisitively at each other.

"I just finished talking to my editor friend. Wait till you see the papers tomorrow. I wish I had bought more of your paintings, Bruno. They're going to become unaffordable after tomorrow."

"We owe you one. You're responsible for this," Bruno said.

"No, you guys are. I just supplied the venue. By the way, the place is free for the next two weeks. Why don't you take some time? I'm sure you could use a break, and Capri is magical."

Bruno and Julian looked at each other and jumped up and down.

"Okay, guys. You're a little old for that kind of enthusiasm," she said dismissively. "But it is cute!" She tugged at Bruno's cheek and then at Julian's.

Bruno leaned over and gave Julian a warm kiss. A flash bulb went off nearby, a reporter snatching an image of them. Bruno and Julian both recoiled at first, an instinctive reaction, an attempt to conceal themselves. They gazed at each other and smiled. Julian wrapped his arms around Bruno's shoulders and turned toward the photographer. They posed, Bruno leaning his head against Julian's.

Two days later, they were laying on chaise lounges at Marianna's pool in Capri.

"*Ma dai*, take that blasted American swimsuit off," Bruno said playfully.

"You first," he replied, eyeing Bruno's Speedo.

With quick abandon, Bruno slipped his off. His brown skin glistened in the Mediterranean sun, and his cock stiffened. Julian slid his hand under the waist band of his suit and slid it down his legs, kicking it off with his feet.

"That's better," he said, tilting his sunglasses down and staring at Julian's taut abdomen. He stood up and approached Julian's chaise, and sat next to him, his buttocks pressed against Julian's side. It was the same provocative gesture he had employed before, but this time, there was no ambiguity.

He rubbed his hand over Julian's smooth chest and ran it affectionately up the side of his face. He rested his hand behind Julian's head and leaned over to give him a warm, moist, and prolonged kiss. It had been over a year since they had last been to Capri. Historically, he would have been long gone, off to a new affair, fleeing his own fear and inadequacies. Occasionally, he felt a flutter in his chest, a small reminder of the vulnerability love represented. He breathed in Julian's scent and felt the solidity of his body under him. He looked out over the landscape, rocky and covered with wild brush. In the distance was the blue horizon, hazy but well defined. He looked intensely at Julian and said, "What a wonderful surprise! I love you so much."

Julian smiled and replied, "*Ti voglio bene!*"

The End

About Author

Michael Hartwig is a Boston and Provincetown base author gaining quick acclaim for his gay romance novels set in exotic places around the world. Stories combine rich descriptions of historical and artistic sites - in places such as the Alps, the Amalfi Coast, and Rome - with steamy love stories where characters grapple with sexual identity at crossroads of their lives. Hartwig's stories weave together facets of his own life – his having lived in Rome, his work as a professor of sexual ethics, and his life as an artist. Plots are fast paced, filled with compelling dialogue, fascinating personalities, and thoughtful exploration of cultural shifts in gender, sexuality, religion, and culture. If you love travel, history, art, romance, and intrigue – you'll love his books!

For More Information and Other Titles Visit: **www.michael-hartwig.com**

CPSIA information can be obtained
at www.ICGtesting.com
Printed in the USA
BVHW080010111121
621200BV00015B/728